Return to Garrison

Kari Wirth

Published by Journey Fiction
Las Vegas, Nevada
www.journeyfiction.com

PRINT ISBN: 978-1-946892-40-9
EBOOK ISBN: 978-1-946892-41-6

Library of Congress Control Number: 2020947641

Journey
Fiction

DEDICATION

Inspiration deserves recognition.
Thank you to the woman who made *Return to Garrison*
possible, my mom, Mary Jo.
I love you.

Prologue

Garrison, Indiana, 2011

The sky spelled doom.

Carl Jenkins clamped down on the bill of his worn out baseball cap, squinting as a gust of wind swooshed across his face. Dark clouds, like billows of smoke from a smoldering fire, had crept in, replacing the blue sky earlier in the day. The ominous sign hovered over the small farming community of Garrison, Indiana. It meant only one thing—a storm was on the way.

After guiding his last milk cow into the barn, Carl called it a day. The short trek up the hill led him to the century-old farmhouse where he saw his wife, Mavis, through the kitchen window, standing in front of the stove.

The wind howled as he walked up the porch's tattered wooden planks and into the house.

"You're just in time," she said, giving the chicken and dumplings a final stir.

"Smells good." He removed his cap and tossed it on the bench in the mudroom, then ran his hand through his thick, matted down hair. Tomorrow was Saturday. He'd go into

5

town to Al Parker's barbershop for a trim in the morning.

Rolling up the sleeves on his red and black flannel shirt, Carl walked to the kitchen sink to wash his hands. He shook off the excess water and reached for a hand towel when a sharp pain surged through his lower back.

"Ouch!"

"Again?" his wife asked.

Hunched over, he winced in pain. "Just twisted it is all. Too fast. I'll be fine."

Mavis sighed as she turned off the stove's burner. "That's the third time this week you 'twisted' it too fast. How many times do I have to tell you to go the doctor and have him check you out?"

"I'll soak in a hot tub after supper," he said, rubbing the kink with his hand. "That'll fix it."

"Carl–"

His hand shot up. "Mavis, please stop. I'll be fine." He scooped up the folded newspaper on the edge of the counter. "Let's eat. I'm starving."

He gently lowered his body into a chair at the kitchen table. Squirming in his seat, he fought to find a comfortable position. He glanced at the newspaper, pretending not to notice his wife pressing her thin lips together as she filled two plates with stew. She set the dishes on the table before returning with a basket of homemade bread sliced into thick chunks.

Carl folded his hands. "Lord, thank you for the food

you've given us. Thank you for the health and strength we'll receive from it. And thank you for blessing us and this farm. In Jesus' name. Amen."

"Amen," Mavis repeated.

Carl unfolded the daily edition of the *Indianapolis Star* and perused the front page articles. He and his wife were halfway through supper when the song coming from the portable radio on the windowsill ended abruptly.

"This is a KJA breaking news weather announcement. A powerful windstorm has made landfall east of Delaware County."

Mavis darted from the table to turn up the volume.

"Gusts are expected to reach up to seventy miles an hour making driving conditions dangerous. Downed power lines and trees have been reported."

"Sounds like a bad one."

Carl looked up. "Uh huh." He put a forkful of dumplings in his mouth and went back to reading the newspaper.

A gust of wind produced an eerie howl. Limbs from the maple tree rattled up and down against the kitchen window.

Carl peeled his attention away from the newspaper and watched Mavis sit down at the table when the lights flickered. He stared at the ceiling, waiting to see if the power would go out.

Mavis clutched her napkin as if it were a security blanket. "Something bad is gonna happen. I feel it."

Carl watched her grip the flimsy material so tightly, tiny pieces of soft paper fell onto the table. He set his fork down. "Ah, hon, don't worry. Those weather guys always make it sound worse than it really is." He reached across the table and gave her hand a good squeeze. "Just finish your dinner."

Staring at the half-eaten portion of food, she pushed her plate away. "I'm not hungry."

With one last scrape of his fork, Carl scooped up what he could of his meal, licked the utensil, and placed it on the plate signaling he was done. He handed the dish to Mavis and picked up the newspaper. "I'm gonna finish reading this on the porch."

"Carl, stay inside. The storm!"

"It ain't gonna hurt me," he said with a chuckle. "Besides, I love watching a good storm."

He walked through the family room toward the front entrance, flipped the switch to the porch light, and stepped outside.

The wind rippled the porch awning, creating a repetitive thudding noise. Carl swayed back and forth on the old porch swing, scanning the newspaper pages from top to bottom.

The warm, humid air gave him a sudden craving for a cup of coffee. *Maybe Mavis would like to join me.* He jerked his head back and chuckled at the absurd notion.

"Coffee inside."

The porch swing creaked when he stood up. In the

8

distance, a pair of headlights pierced the darkness.

The car sped down the road, much faster than the 45 mile per hour limit. He watched the vehicle skid past the sharp corner rounding out County Road. The noise from the whipping winds didn't drown out the sound of squealing tires as the car violently fishtailed.

Carl wanted to call out to the driver, but nothing came out of his mouth. Helplessly, he watched the green Grand Am slam into a tree.

He raced down the porch steps and across the front yard as hail the size of gumballs pelted his body. But he didn't care.

The car was a mangled piece of metal. He tugged on the door handle. "Come on!" Grunting with his teeth clenched, he tried again, praying the door would open. "Please, God! Come on! Come on!" But the driver's door was jammed shut.

He yanked on the handle again, but the force he exerted triggered pain in his back as if someone stabbed him with a knife. He screamed, pressing his hands on his lower back. Struggling to catch his breath, he collapsed against the car.

Carl pounded on the cracked window, hoping the noise would rouse the driver slumped over the steering wheel. Cupping his hands around his eyes like a pair of binoculars and squinting through the hail, he still couldn't make out who it was. Using his hand like a windshield wiper, he pushed the wet surface back and forth to get a clearer picture inside the totaled car. A thick strand of long, dark hair lay across the woman's face.

He gasped when he recognized her. "No! It can't be."

His head tilted up at the sound of wood cracking. One snap. Then another. By the third crack, he watched in horror as the winds uprooted a tree that plummeted onto the roof of the car, grabbing black wires from the electric pole with it on its decent.

Carl dove to the ground, shielding his head from the sparks shooting from the car's engine like a mini fireworks display.

He stumbled to his feet.

Live wires draped over the crushed car ignited flames beneath the hood. The fire spread quickly. Flames leaped onto his shirt, scorching the fabric. Fiercely, he slapped his arm.

Seconds later, the fire set off an explosion, engulfing the car in roaring flames.

The blast sent Carl flying. When he hit the ground, his head made contact with something hard and his vision blurred. His fingers dug into the cold, wet dirt as he tried lifting his chest off the ground. But what little strength he had wasn't enough and his body collapsed.

Chapter One

Buffalo, New York, 2019

Anna's gut twisted in a knot the size of a tennis ball. The sight of her associate producer, Tracy, powerwalking into the control room was never a good sign. A yellow piece of paper waived wildly in her hand. "This just came in." She handed Anna the sheet with scribbled shorthand notes only news producers understood. "A crew is at the scene. Joel is going live."

"Thanks."

Anna didn't waste any time typing a lead into the teleprompter. Glancing up at a small screen on the wall labeled *Remote 2* in the upper right-hand corner, she watched Joel Brewster run his hand over his blond hair, gently patting down the sides. A model for the runway or a reporter? Hard to decipher.

She snorted in disgust. *If his head gets any bigger, it won't fit on the screen.*

She leaned toward the microphone and shouted in his earpiece. "Give me a mic check!"

He answered as he continued grooming, smoothing his blue speckled tie against his white dress shirt. "Check one, two, three." In the background, four police cars flashed their red and blue lights. Anna couldn't help but notice how the yellow caution tape Joel stood in front of set off the blue of his pinstripe suit.

"Stand by." She looked at the director. "Don, ready with the graphic?"

"Ready, Anna. We're coming out of commercial in thirty."

Leaning toward the microphone, she read an abridged version of the story to the five o'clock anchors. "Bill, Suzanne, we've got breaking news. Two men held up a bank, a dye pack exploded, they got pulled over, led police on a chase, ended with a crash. Lead is in the prompter. Joel is standing by."

"Got it," they said in unison, jotting down notes on their scripts.

The commercial ended, and Don started the countdown. "Here we go in three, two, one."

The words "BREAKING NEWS" in red capitalized letters glided across the middle of the screen. Suzanne read the first half of the lead. "This story is happening right now. Police tell Channel 3 News a bold pair of bank robbers were caught red-handed and sent a fellow officer on a wild chase before their run from the law came to a terrifying halt."

The suspects were pulled from the wrecked vehicle and handcuffed. *Great video!* Joel pressed his finger on his earpiece, nodding his head when he heard Anna point out the photo op.

Bill finished the lead. "Joel Brewster is live at the scene of this horrific crash. Joel, what happened out there?"

"Bill and Suzanne, as you can see," he said, stepping outside the shot, "the two suspects are being taken into police custody as we speak." The camera followed the two men as they were escorted to another squad car while Joel continued his report.

"Police tell me around four thirty this afternoon, those two men held up the Summit Financial Bank on Dryer and East. They were given a bag full of money containing dye packs and took off. Buffalo Police Officer Rudy Gore pulled the suspects over for speeding and saw the ink stained bag and cash on the floor. That's when the suspects fled, setting off a high-speed chase that lasted about ten minutes. From what I'm being told, the chase had Officer Gore going up to seventy miles per hour before the suspects lost control of their vehicle, side-swiped a row of parked cars, and then Officer Gore crashed into the suspects."

Leaning into the microphone, Anna fed Bill a question for the reporter. "Ask how the officer is doing."

The anchor complied. "Joel, how's Officer Gore? Is he okay?"

The reporter slid back into the shot. "Bill, I've been told he's banged up but conscience. He gave a thumbs-up when the paramedics put him on the gurney. He's on his way to Erie County Medical Center. Coming up at six, I'll be talking to the doctors about his condition."

Suzanne finished the report with an impromptu, "We're all hoping for the best. Thanks, Joel for the update. We'll check in with you in just a bit. Onto other news..."

Anna's head bounced back and forth between the two television screens like a ping-pong ball. She watched her competitors' newscasts, hoping her team finished the race first. "Does six or eight have it, Don?"

"Nope."

"Are you sure?"

"Yeah, first again. Great job on spotting the suspects."

"Thanks."

The newscast returned to the original agenda without a hiccup in the rest of the hour-long show.

As Bill gave his signature sign off, "Thanks for joining us. For Suzanne, myself, and all of us here at Channel 3 News, good night," Anna left the control room and headed for newsroom.

She grabbed her purse from her desk drawer, threw her spring jacket around her shoulders, and walked toward the exit. The faster she got out of there, the sooner she'd get home.

To make a clean getaway, she had to move—and fast. No stopping to chitchat. No wondering about the story breaking over the police scanner. Just get her stuff and go. The first rule in avoiding conversation—never make eye contact. So, when she glanced in Tracy's direction, she instantly knew she'd made a mistake.

Maybe she didn't see me.

"Anna! Hey, wait up!"

Nope.

"Way to hustle out there."

Anna's eyebrows scrunched together. "What do you mean?"

"The robbery, silly."

"Oh, right. That."

Anna wasn't in the mood for accolades or having to look at Tracy's tooth grin.

"Can you believe those guys? Robbing a bank in broad daylight. I mean, come on! I just can't believe it!"

The newsroom rookie had only been on the job three weeks. She was still flying high after landing her first entry-level position out of college. It wouldn't be long before the honeymoon phase dissipated.

"Yeah, people do stupid things." Anna glanced at her watch. She'd be pulling out of the parking lot by now if it wasn't for gabby gums.

"I never knew TV news could be so exciting! I get the info. You spot the crooks." She winked. "We make a great team, don't you think?"

"Sure, Tracy. Hey, listen, I have to go. I'm late for...uh, an appointment."

"Oh, okay." She waved her hand in front of her face, giving her permission to walk away before calling out, "We'll talk about it more tomorrow!"

Anna worked her arms through her jacket sleeves as she headed toward the hallway where she nearly collided into Bill.

"Whoa there!" His arms shot up to his chest, shielding her from impact.

"Sorry about that," she said, fumbling with her collar.

He cocked his chiseled chin in the air. "Made me look good out there again. Just what I like." He dumped his script into the recycling bin next to the copier like it was last-night's leftovers.

She turned her head, looking over her shoulder just enough to make eye contact. "Anytime, Bill."

Suzanne chimed in. "Anna is the best." The tall brunette flashed an appreciative smile and walked past her.

The best at what? Writing a few lines, telling people what to say and where to stand?

She glanced at her watch again. Sighing, she threw her purse over her shoulder and made a beeline for the door.

Pulling out of the gated parking lot in her black Jeep Cherokee, Anna had only one thing on her mind.

Three flights up the narrow stairs, Anna's stomach let out an audible gurgle. The aroma seeping from the Panera Bread bag in her hand didn't make it any easier on her hunger pains.

Once inside her studio apartment, she hung up her jacket in the closet and put her purse on the couch before sitting on the folding chair at her desk in the middle of the open living area.

Biting into the turkey and avocado sandwich, she fired up her laptop. Time for her second job—writing a book. The clock was ticking. Three hours of solid work to do before calling it a day.

Anna shoved a forkful of Cobb salad into her mouth and waited anxiously for the desktop screen to appear.

She opened a saved document and read the words on the screen over and over. But the food next to the computer was much more appealing. The more she stared at it, the hungrier she got. She needed nourishment to get the creative juices flowing. Before she knew it, she'd polished off the sandwich and scrapped up the last bit of dressing-soaked lettuce in the container.

Dinner was done. Back to work.

An hour later, all Anna had to show for it was a page of mental notes she'd taken during the day that sounded better in her head than the gibberish on the screen. Everyone has a breaking point. At that moment, she hit hers.

"Garbage! Nothing but GARBAGE!" Her fists slammed on top of the desk.

The words on the screen morphed into an elite army on enemy lines. She was outnumbered. They had to go. The whole battalion. Pressing the delete key hard enough to pop it off, she watched sentences vanish at warp speed. In a matter of seconds, fifteen pages no longer existed.

A surge of relief ran through her body, but only for a moment.

What am I doing? This is never going to work.

Anna's futile attempt at writing a book in her spare time proved a painful realization. The options were few. Her choice—only one.

Now, she was ready to do something about it.

Chapter Two

Ten minutes into her shift, Anna managed to peel herself out of the chair.

Her heart pounded twice as fast as usual, pressing against her body, trying to break free and leap out of her chest. With each step she took toward her boss's office, a thumping pulsated in her ears. She swore everyone around her heard it too.

She knocked on the open office door. No turning back now. "Got a second, Sarah?"

The middle-aged brunette looked up, balancing the phone receiver on her elevated shoulder while Anna stood in the doorway, internally rehearsing her lines like an actress.

Sarah waved her hand, motioning for Anna to come in.

She took a deep breath, stepped inside, and shut the door before dragging a chair from the corner of the office to sit in.

Sarah held up her index finger and mouthed, *One minute.*

Anna nodded, forcing her lips into a smile. She waited for her boss to end the phone call and found distraction by studying mounds of folders, three piles of papers, and old videotapes scattered across the desk.

"I don't care how much it's going to cost in overtime, we need to cover the story," Sarah said to the person on the other end of the phone. "Tell Joel he's got to pull a double. He's the big reporter with the big paycheck. This is his job."

If she's ticked now, wait until she hears what I have to say.

"Owen. We...have...an exclusive." Her demanding tone rose to a singsong octave becoming softer as if she were speaking to an unruly child. "If we wait and the other stations get wind of it, we'll wind up with egg on our face and you know what? I hate eggs. Get what I'm saying?"

A moment of silence passed before her rose-colored lips stretched out to a satisfied smile. "Good. I'm glad we agree. Make it happen." She hung up the phone without saying goodbye and started typing an email. "One disaster down, and it's not even ten o'clock."

"Is that the councilman embezzlement case you've been working on?"

"Yeah, I couldn't sit on it any longer." Sarah's eyes were glued to the computer screen, and her fingers flew across the keyboard even as she spoke. "Three sources willing to go on camera and documented proof. I can't wait to nail this guy. These politicians make me sick. All the money they make, and they still stick their greedy little hands in the cookie jar." She finished her email and sent it with an authoritative click. "So, what's up?"

A lump formed in Anna's throat. She swallowed past it. "I need to talk to you."

20

"Shoot."

"I've been thinking...and I've decided–"

A brief knock and the heavy oak door swung open. A young woman barged in, uninvited.

"Mrs. Cunningham, here are the ratings from yesterday. I highlighted each of the three stations to make it easier to read." She proudly handed the sheet to Sarah.

Brown-noser.

"Thanks, Casey."

Casey Pollen, the station's summer intern. Anna crossed her arms and glared at the perky nuisance. The way she sashayed through the newsroom in ruffled miniskirts and low-cut shirts like she was part of the crew drove her nuts. But she didn't fool Anna. Casey didn't care about the work put in at the station. She was just there to collect her college credits.

"If you need anything else, Mrs. Cunningham, I'll be searching the national wires for stories we can localize."

Anna let out an absurd snort. The only thing Casey looked at was her reflection in the small compact she carried around in her purse. Her hands spent more time fixing her bleach-blond hair than they did on the computer. Then there was the makeup fascination. Coating her lips with layers of sticky bubble gum colored gloss, then running her tongue across her top row of teeth.

Spinning around on the tippy toes of her stiletto heels, she waived at Anna like a sorority sister and shut the door as she left the office. Sadly, Sarah couldn't fire an unpaid intern. But Casey was good for one thing—answering the phone.

"Oh, great, look at this!" The news director shouted as she flicked the sheet with her finger. "We slipped two points during the six o'clock." Her countenance quickly changed the farther she read. "But we did jump from an eighteen to a twenty at eleven."

Anna leaned across the desk to sneak a peek. "That's great," she said, throwing in a half-smile for extra insurance.

Using her finger as a guide across the page, Sarah compared numbers with the competition. "Channel 6 has been nipping at our heels for months." She tapped her pen against the sheet as a wrinkle formed in her forehead. "Not the way I want to head into May Sweeps. Thank God, the five is holding strong."

She held the sheet across the desk. "Look, a twenty-six to start and you finished with a thirty-four. Whatever you're doing, keep doing it."

Just what I needed. Why couldn't she yell at me like she did Owen? It would make having to tell her much easier. If only that Barbie clone hadn't barged in.

Anna wiped her clammy hands against her black pants. "Sarah, I need to talk to you. It's important."

The tips of her eyebrows met in the middle of her forehead. Inching closer, leaning in as if she was ready to hear a deep, dark secret, she asked, "Is something wrong?"

Anna maintained eye contact, fighting the urge to look away. "W-well, it's um..." Her voice trailed off. Glancing down at her hands, she watched her fingers fidget with one another. She couldn't stop them.

"What is it?" Sarah's eyes shifted from intrigue to concern.

"I don't know how to tell you this."

"Yeah?"

"I'm...leaving the station. This is my two-weeks' notice."

Staring at each other, waiting for the other to make the first move, an awkward silence fell over the room, the kind that made a minute seem like an hour. Then, like a thunderstorm unleashing torrential rain, Sarah snapped. "What? You can't leave!"

And here it comes.

"You're my best producer. See!" She waved the ratings sheet in Anna's face.

"You didn't think I'd be here forever, did you? Besides, you can fill my spot by morning."

Sarah slammed the sheet down on the desk. "I don't want another producer."

She stood so fast it sent her black leather chair rolling away, stopping inches before hitting the wall. Hands planted on her hips, head shaking, she paced back and forth.

Anna rubbed her hand against her forehead. "Can you let me explain?"

Sarah's hands flew up in surrender. "Okay, okay." She rolled the chair back to the edge of the desk and sat down. Sliding a stack of papers off to the side, she clasped her hands together. "Channel 6 offered you a better position, didn't they?"

"No."

"Are you sick? Like terminally ill kind of sick?"

"No." Agitation coated Anna's tone.

"Then it's money. It has to be. I can give you a raise. I'll have a small fight on my hands with corporate, but you know me. I love going up against the big boys."

"It's not the money, Sarah."

"Then for goodness sake, what is it?"

"I've been doing the same job for eight years. The monotony is killing me. I don't want to wake up in twenty years still screaming in Joel's earpiece to give me a mic check."

"You're in a rut. It happens. But I'm sure we can come up with a way for you to stay and feel more fulfilled."

An offer she couldn't refuse. Not possible.

Sarah clapped her hands together, impressed with her solution. "I'll make you executive producer. A bump in pay, plus more say about what goes on air. And, you'll be in management."

Looking at her boss, aggressiveness rose up. Anna knew what she wanted and she wasn't afraid to say it. "You don't get it. There's got to be more to life than this. More than these four dismal walls closing in on me. I'm suffocating, Sarah. I need to get out and breathe."

"What is it that you want? Because I hate to burst your bubble, hon. Most jobs are just that. Jobs."

Anna sighed. "I'm writing a book."

Sarah's wide-eyed stare was hard to interpret. "A book?" she repeated. "That's what this is about? A book?" She chuckled. "Anna, you can still write a book without quitting your job. No one's stopping you."

"Yes, someone is."

"Who?"

Anna catapulted out of her seat. "This place! You. Me. Everything! I've tried for months. It's not working."

"So that's why you've been bolting out of here every night like a car at the Indy 500?"

"That noticeable?"

"Look, you're great at what you do. Every–"

Anna cut her off before she could finish. "It's not enough, Sarah. I'm not happy. I'm thirty years old, and I don't have a lot to show for it."

The light bulb went off. "This is about more than writing a book, isn't it?"

Anna sat back down. "Maybe."

Sarah leaned back in the chair with her hands clasped against her midsection. "What if your book doesn't make it to the shelves? Hmm? What if you walk away from everything and all your work was for nothing? Then what?"

"Then... I'll be heartbroken. I'll be a failure. I'll wallow over all the time I spent on it. But I won't regret taking a chance. To finally step out and take a risk. I've wanted to write a book since I was a kid. But somewhere along the way I lost my vision and settled for good enough. I'm done with good enough. It's time for me to go."

Sarah sighed. "You know I can't keep your job open for you."

"I don't expect you to."

A crooked smile appeared on her face. "Guess there's nothing else left to say."

"So, you're okay? With me leaving?"

"I didn't say that. But I can't stop you either." Sarah stood up, walked to the front of her desk with her arms opened wide, and hugged Anna. "Good luck, honey."

Relief swept over Anna like a refreshing rain after a long drought. A surge of excitement ran through her at the thought of diving into her book with hours upon hours at her disposal. Everything was going to work out.

At least, that's what she thought.

Chapter Three

If the portable air conditioner in Anna's apartment hadn't gone kaput three days earlier, the window unit would have been a lifesaver, rescuing her from an unseasonable May heat wave. She should've made the ten-minute drive to Home Depot to buy a new one, but didn't. A decision she regretted as she sat at her desk waving a spiral-bound notebook back and forth in a pathetic attempt to cool down.

The white tank top she wore stuck to her moist skin like glue. Even her blue running shorts felt like a burlap sack around her waist. Hoping for a breeze, she walked to the Victorian window in the living room and hoisted the heavy structure.

She tugged at the hair tie around her wrist before finally pulling her shoulder-length hair up in a ponytail as she returned to the desk. Sitting down on the chair Sarah gave her as a going away present, Anna squirmed from side to side as her skin stuck to the black leather.

As she picked up a cup of hot green tea next to the laptop, the thin slice of lemon floating on the surface bobbed from side to side. She took a sip, savoring the moment the beverage hit her lips until she swallowed while rereading the last paragraph she wrote.

Time to get back to work.

Two weeks had passed since Anna left Channel 3 News to work full-time on her book. She only had two chapters done.

The first morning she woke up without help from an alarm clock was like a dream. She imagined watching her fingers fly across the keyboard faster than the thoughts coming to her brain, cranking out page after page. The plot, the characters, the dialogue, the conclusion—all the pieces of a great story that had been locked away like prisoners and now were being set free.

Anna's love for reading started at a young age. She'd always loved curling up with a good book to escape reality and get lost in someone else's world, just for a little while. Cozy beneath the sheet and blanket of her bed, holding a small flashlight in one hand and a book in the other, her mother often caught her reading when she was supposed to be sleeping.

"Lights out, sweetheart," she'd say as she peeked her head around the doorway of her daughter's bedroom.

Her soft-spoken words echoed in Anna's head. She closed her eyes to get a clearer picture of her mother's long dark hair dangling past her shoulders. No one would've guessed she worked behind a stove all day.

At the sound of her sweet voice, Anna's head would pop up. "Just a few more minutes, Momma, please?"

Her brown eyes stared back kindly at her daughter.

"Well, okay. Five more minutes, then it's time to go to sleep."

She'd always go back in the bedroom to tuck Anna in, gently tugging the bed sheet up close to her daughter's chin. Leaning down, careful not to wake her, she delicately kissed her forehead and softly ran her hand over her hair sprawled out on the pillow. The scent of her mother's mango-peach lotion lingered in the room as Anna drifted off to sleep.

As Anna closed her eyes, the same scent washed over her as if her mother were standing next to her.

Pounding her fists onto the desk, Anna whined, "Why can't I do this?"

Writing a suspense novel should've been easy. It was her favorite genre. She must have read hundreds of them over the years.

"Stop. Write. Just write anything!" she shouted. "Even if it doesn't make any sense, write and edit later." She nodded. "Yeah, write and edit later."

Obeying her command, Anna started typing. The pressure valve opened. The sound of fingertips striking the keyboard echoed throughout the room, bouncing off the cathedral ceiling. The rhythmic beat was music to her ears. Words formed sentences, and sentences turned into paragraphs.

Progress, finally!

A brief pause to gather her thoughts and she was ready to start the next scene in the chapter. She had to keep typing.

As she placed her fingertips on the second row of keys, her momentum came to a screeching halt when fire truck sirens blasted by outside.

Exposing her teeth, growling like a watchdog ready to attack an intruder, she got up and slammed the window shut. Yes, it would be warmer inside the apartment. She couldn't control the heat, but she could put up a barrier to block the outside noises.

She plopped down in the chair and anchored her bare feet to the hardwood floor as she pushed the piece of furniture forward.

Calm down, just calm down. Her fingers hovered over the keyboard, like a pianist about to perform.

She couldn't remember what she was going to type. "Think Anna, think."

Hitting the Page Up key, the cursor soared to the top of the page. Rereading the previous paragraph might trigger her memory.

Thirty-three-year-old Derek Marshall hopped into his black Porsche. His butler stood in the doorway. "Don't wait up, Lyle," he said with a cocky grin and sped away from his gated Beverly Hills mansion. On his way to pick up his date Marisa—the new flavor of the week—the powerful heir to a multi-billion-dollar software company reached into his inner coat pocket and pulled out a flask, unscrewed the cap, and finished what was left of the whisky. He pulled into the driveway and turned off the ignition. He took one last look at his hair in the rearview mirror, got out of the car, and walked to the front door. He rang the bell. Nothing. He rang the bell again. Still no sign of his date. He knocked on the door. It was already opened. The creaking sound startled him. He carefully pushed on the door. "Marisa? It's me, Derek." He stepped inside the pitch black entrance. Searching for the light switch, he found it. He flicked the switch and wished he hadn't when he saw...

The trick worked. Suddenly, the clever phrase popped back into Anna's head. She smiled and started typing when her cell phone rang. She slapped her forehead, angry that she had forgotten to put it on silent.

Ignore it.

But she couldn't. The constant noise sent chills up her spine like fingernails dragging across a chalkboard. Her hands squeezed the sides of her forehead. Quickly, she answered the call. "Hello?"

No response.

"Hello?" Still nothing. "Hello? Is anybody there?"

There were muffled background noises before a young woman said, "Good evening, ma'am. Is this Miss Sutton?"

"Yeah," she replied, waiting to hear what the unknown caller wanted.

"My name is Chelsea, Miss Sutton, and I am calling on behalf of Frontier Mortgages."

Great, a telemarketer. Why didn't I just let the phone ring?

Before Anna could say she wasn't interested, the woman continued. "I want to let you in on an exciting opportunity where you can lower your monthly rate by fifteen percent."

No doubt the sales pitch came from a piece of paper hanging in the woman's dinky cubicle. Anna could practically hear her supervisor say, "Just follow the script. Just follow the script." The one and only real instruction to the group of minimum wage workers.

"Miss Sutton, all you have to do is take the next couple minutes to answer a few questions. Shall we begin?"

"Chelsea? It is Chelsea?" Anna clarified sarcastically. "I got a question for you."

"Certainly ma'am, go right ahead."

"How can I lower my mortgage rate when I don't even have a mortgage? My address is right in front of your face. Are you blind that you can't see an apartment number follows the street address? I'm just guessing but that should be your first clue, Sherlock, that I *do not* own a house!"

Chelsea's voice trembled. "Oh...Miss Sutton, I'm sorry I bothered you."

"Yeah, well you did." Anna hung up, switched the ringer to silent, and tossed the phone onto the table.

She'd been mean and incredibly rude, but she didn't care.

Standing in the middle of the living room with her fists clenched at her sides, she peered up at the ceiling. She closed her eyes, opened her mouth, and let out a scream so loud, the walls were on the brink of shaking.

The blood-curdling yell left her struggling to breathe. Her chest heaved as she gasped for oxygen. She needed to vent. It was the only thing she could think to do.

After a few minutes, Anna regained her composure. She was ready to get back to work. But rage returned with a fury at the sound of a soft knock. She abruptly opened the door. "WHAT?"

Her elderly landlord stood in the hallway wearing pink, furry slippers and a floral housecoat.

Anna swiped away a strand of hair hanging over her eye. "Oh. Hi, Mrs. Elardo."

"Hello there, dear. Are you okay?" She peeked around her shoulder to get a glimpse inside the apartment, but Anna stepped to the right to block her view.

"I'm fine, why do you ask?"

"I was watching my favorite television show, *I Love Lucy*. Channel 52 has an *I Love Lucy* marathon on all this week."

Anna threw the old woman a bone. "Is that right?"

"Yes. Tonight, she and Ethel are in the candy factory. You know which episode I'm talking about, don't you, dear?"

"Yeah, Mrs. Elardo, I've seen it." *Get on with it already.*

"I just love that episode," she said, clapping her hands in delight. "Where was I? Oh, yes, so they're shoveling all this chocolate in their mouths and in their clothes, then all of the sudden, I heard a scream." She pointed to Anna. "It came from your apartment.

More like, why did you scream, eh, Mrs. Elardo?

"I didn't even turn off the TV. I scooted up here as fast as I could and here I am. Did you hurt yourself?"

"Well...I, uh..."

The silver-haired lady stared intently, eager to find out what happened in apartment number three. Gripping her hands, waiting for a response, if her eyes could speak, they'd say, "Go on, I'm listening."

Anna's eyes landed on the sloppy bun of hair placed high on top of the woman's head. But what really caught her attention was the barrage of bobby pins scattered randomly throughout the chunk of hair.

"You were saying, dear?"

"My foot... I hit it...against the coffee table," Anna said. "Boy, did it ever hurt. Still does." She bent down and rubbed her ankle. "Woo, did it hurt."

"Do you need me to call an ambulance? It might be sprained, or worse, broken right in half."

The old woman bought it.

"Na, it's just bruised. Ice will bring down the swelling." Politely, Anna started to shut the door. "Thanks, good night."

But the landlord's quick reflexes stopped the door in mid-motion. "Aren't you going to get some ice, dear?"

So close.

"Ice. Right."

Mrs. Elardo positioned herself in the doorway. The pressure was on for Anna to put on an Oscar worthy performance. Taking a few steps toward the refrigerator, she threw in a fake limp. She reached inside the freezer and held up a frozen sack. "Ice," she announced and limped back to the door, wincing and letting out a few ouches.

She stared at Mrs. Elardo, hoping she would leave.

"Well, I really should ice this foot."

"Oh, okay, dear. Yes, I have to go too. In the next episode, Lucy goes to Italy and stomps the grapes! I just love that Lucy!" she said, chuckling at the thought of the redheaded comedian.

"Sounds like fun."

The old woman's hazel eyes grew wide. She snapped her boney fingers. "Say, would you like to join me?"

The last thing Anna wanted to do was watch a bunch of black and white reruns. She had work to do.

"That's nice of you, but I should really ice this foot," she replied, holding up the pack.

"You could ice it while we watch TV. I'll prop your foot up for you and everything. It's no trouble!"

"Thanks, Mrs. Elardo, but I'm getting kind of tired. I think I'm ready to call it a night."

The landlord's smile dropped. "Oh. Okay. Maybe some other time, dear."

"Sure. Good night."

"Good night."

Without a moment to hesitate, Anna shut the door. The cold sensation from the ice pack reminded her about the frozen bag. She went to the refrigerator and opened the freezer. Glancing at the ice pack, she chucked it inside and slammed the door shut.

Chapter Four

Jake O'Connor couldn't wait to get out of the house.

He hoisted his green backpack off his unmade bed and slung it over his shoulder as three cans of spray paint clanked together. Just as he was ready to leave, his cell phone vibrated. He viewed the caller ID before answering. It was Bryce.

"Hey man. Yeah, I got them. See you in few." He ended the call and stuck the phone in the front pocket of his baggy jeans.

Heading for the door, he tripped over the paper-thin blue bedspread sagging on the floor, but regained his balance before hitting the ground face first. He stepped around piles of clean and dirty clothes without a thought to pick them up or put them away. Jake took one last look at the only room in the house where he had some privacy and softly closed the door behind him.

From the first floor hallway, Jake got a clear view of the family room. Marty and Sam were slouched on the brown couch while Holly looked like a ball with her legs tucked up to her chest on the reclining chair.

The teens stared blankly at the television screen waiting for the season finale of *NCIS*. The crime solving drama served as the perfect distraction, making Jake's stealthy exit that much easier.

He quickly walked past the wide family room entrance. A loud squeak sprang up from the worn hardwood floor, stopping him dead in his tracks. The noise startled him, but the three teens didn't even flinch.

The weight from the spray paint cans in the backpack sent the strap slowly down his shoulder. Delicately, he pulled the sack up. The front door was within his sights. Just a few more feet and he was home free.

A grin spread across his thin, long face at the thought of a successful escape until he heard a voice coming from the kitchen.

"I don't care what your excuse is, you know the rules."

A chill ran up his spine. The woman's voice was unmistakable.

He stared at the front door, longing to be on the other side of it. All he had to do was keep walking. But curiosity won, sending him toward the kitchen to see who Stephanie Grey was chewing out this time.

Jake inched his way across the narrow hallway. If he were caught leaving the house without permission, he wouldn't see daylight for a month.

Gripping the edge of the wall, he peeked around the corner and into the kitchen. He stood stiff as a statue, hoping not to lose his balance as he held onto the wall tight enough to turn his knuckles white.

All he saw was Stephanie's backside.

What's she doing here? Where's Tina or the other girl... What's her name? Mandy.

Towering five feet, nine inches with her head cocked down, the forty-year-old woman stood in front of Jasmine.

Jake's overgrown hair fell diagonally across his eyes, blocking his view. He let out a slow breath, forcing a puff of air up toward his bangs. Loosening his grip on the wall, his eyes fixated on Jasmine's dark brown hair and bronze skin. He often daydreamed about having her as his girlfriend. Images flashed through his mind: walking in the school hallways holding her hand; meeting her at her locker after each class. Imagining the feel of her sweet, pouty lips against his sent his teenage hormones into overdrive. Unfortunately, the closest he'd come to making skin-to-skin contact with Jasmine was one night during dinner when she asked him to pass the butter and her hand accidently brushed up against his.

Jake's fantasy was interrupted as Stephanie continued her rant.

"Weeknight curfew is seven o'clock. You knew that the first day you came here, and it hasn't changed just because *you* have a job."

"I'm sorry," Jasmine said, her voice just above a whisper. Her head hung as her hair fell across her face. "My boss needed me to stay. Sal didn't show up, and Jenny went home sick."

"Why didn't you call? It takes two seconds to make a phone call."

Jasmine shrugged her shoulders. "I don't know."

"That's not an acceptable answer. A smart girl like you knows better." Stephanie's hands bounced off her hips. "You've given me no choice. This little incident cost you your weekend pass."

"But I'm going camping and horseback riding in Ellicottville with Morgan and her parents."

"Not this weekend you aren't."

"Please, Stephanie, don't do this. I promise I'll call next time. I'll never miss curfew again. Please!"

"Too late. Rules develop and strengthen character. Rules keep you safe."

Tears fell down Jasmine's face.

"Hopefully next time, you'll think about what transpired tonight before you act or don't act."

The teen's lower lip quivered between sniffles and choked-up sobs. "But I– I've never been horseback riding before. I–"

Stephanie's hand flew up, silencing Jasmine. "This is the only way you'll truly reform."

Reform? Jake shook his head in disbelief. *What a witch.*

"Now get upstairs and get ready for bed."

Jasmine wiped the tears from her face. "It's only eight o'clock."

Her reply didn't faze Stephanie. "I know. Now go."

Jasmine turned around and took the staircase in the kitchen to the second floor, stomping on each step as Stephanie followed her. Once they were out of sight, Jake didn't waste another second. His window of opportunity had shrunk. He headed for the front door, squeezing through the entrance without making a sound.

Finally outside, he sighed in relief and hurried to the red Mustang waiting across the street.

The driver's side door opened, and he crawled in the back seat. No hellos were exchanged. Grabbing a beer from the case next to him, Jake twisted off the cap and took a swig. Before he could swallow, the sound of squealing tires echoed in the street.

Chapter Five

Sprawled out on the couch, Anna massaged her temples to avert the headache she felt coming on. She had wasted hours upon hours in front of the computer screen. Early morning, afternoon, late evening, she'd tried it all. Nothing made a difference. But the interruptions of the night made her wake up and take notice. Her plan wasn't working out.

She entertained the notion of crawling back to Channel 3 News, begging for her job back. The mundane producer position made her cringe. She imagined the phony smiles from her colleagues, welcoming her back. The whispers circulating the newsroom about her failed venture. Then Sarah's caveat shot back at her like a boomerang. *You know I can't keep your job open for you.*

Anna sat up covered in a cold sweat, her breathing shallow.

What have I done?

She gripped the edge of couch, squeezing the polyester fabric, hoping for a sign to give her clarity on what to do next. Tucked away in a white basket was the sign she needed.

Drawn to the object, Anna went to the corner of the

living room. She squatted, her knees cracking on the way down. She sat on the floor next to the canvas container she'd bought on clearance from Wal-Mart while grocery shopping one Saturday afternoon. Old magazines and books hid a large white photo album propped up against the back of the basket. Years had gone by since she'd thumbed through the book, enough years to make her forget it existed. With a swift yank, she pulled it out of the basket and gazed at it as if it had some sort of magical spell on her. She wiped a thin layer of dust from the cover with her palm, then carefully opened the thick album.

The pages were filled with pictures of her from the time she was a baby to her early twenties. She studied each photograph, pondering details of when and why it was taken. Holidays, school functions, and silly candid poses that still made her chuckle. One by one, fond childhood memories warmed her heart. But one photo captivated her attention.

The seven-year-old girl sported a pink tank top and jean shorts. Her thick, brown hair was pulled up in a ponytail, the same way Anna's hair was at that moment.

She remembered the intense heat that afternoon had made for a hot and muggy day in the Midwest. She and her mother were heading to Cedar Point for their first family vacation. They hadn't left town yet when she stopped the car to take her first picture. Anna posed like a future runway model with her hands on her hips and head cocked to the side. Her beaming smile exposed two missing teeth. The billboard sign behind her read, **WELCOME TO GARRISON, INDIANA**, in thick uppercase letters and *A Friendly Town* underneath in a fancy cursive.

Staring at the photograph made Anna's throat dry up. She swallowed hard.

Was Garrison the answer?

Immediately, she shook her head and slammed the album shut. Buffalo was home, not Garrison. Not anymore. But like a criminal returning to the scene of the crime, she opened the book again, quickly flipping through the pages to find the picture. She had to be sure she wasn't getting caught up in the emotion of it all.

Garrison? Could it be?

Returning to her hometown after an eight year absence seemed absurd. Almost absurd enough to work.

Chapter Six

The ringing phone woke Claire Hartman from a deep sleep. In her groggy state, she glanced at the alarm clock on the nightstand, her half-opened eyes working extra hard to focus on the blurry, neon red numbers.

"Ten thirty," she mumbled. "Who in the world's calling?"

The annoying ring aroused her curiosity, unlike her husband, Denny, who continued snorting and snoring in between heavy breaths. She flung off the sheet and sat up on the edge of the bed. A squeak from the mattress spring ensued when she stood up to leave the bedroom.

The ringing grew louder as she made her way down the hall, running her hand along the wall for support. She let out a shocked hiss when her bare feet hit the cold, linoleum floor, and goosebumps tickled her bare arm as she snatched the receiver from the wall mounted phone.

"Hello?"

"Hi." The voice on the line hesitated. "It's me."

Claire's eyes opened wide. "Anna? Is that you, darlin'?" she asked in a drawn-out accent.

"Yeah, it's me."

"Well ain't this a surprise! It was worth getting up just to hear your voice."

"It's good to hear yours, too. How's Denny?"

"Oh, the same. You know Denny. Stubborn as a mule, sweet as a gumdrop."

Anna chuckled. "How are things at the diner?"

"Business is business, I guess."

"No news is good news. Or, so they say, right?"

"Yeah. Yeah, that's what they say," she repeated. "So, wanna tell me what's goin' on?"

"What do you mean?"

"Anna Marie Sutton, I've known you since the day you came out of your momma's belly," Claire fired back, her voice escalating. "I may not be the sharpest tool in the shed, but I know when something ain't right. And something ain't right. Now... let's start again." She paused, her tone calm. "What's goin' on?"

"Claire?" She sounded offended.

"Don't, Claire me. I haven't heard from you in years. Now, outta the blue, you just had to call me wondering about the diner? And so late!" She blew out an absurd sigh.

For a moment, Claire wondered if Anna would say anything, but she finally blurted out, "I quit my job."

"You did what?"

"I quit my job."

"To take another one?"

"Not really. I don't have a job anymore."

"Why in the world would you go and do a thing like that?" she shouted.

"I'm finally writing my book."

Claire sighed. "Well, that's great, darlin', but you need to work. How do you suppose you're gonna live?"

"I have enough money saved up. Enough for at least three months. Maybe more." Anna paused. "Actually, that's why I called."

"Uh-huh. I figured there was something you weren't telling me. Smart girl like you wouldn't just up and quit her job without a plan. So, what is it?"

"I– I'm coming to Garrison."

Claire was speechless.

"Did you hear what I said?"

"I heard you." She kept her tone light, almost afraid that if she got too excited she'd spook Anna into changing her mind.

"This isn't the reaction I expected."

"You're coming home? You're really coming home, Anna?"

"Yeah. I guess I am."

The confirmation was all she needed. "You're coming home!" Claire shouted. "I just knew you couldn't stay away forever."

"Before you get too excited, Claire, it's just for the summer. I can't get any work done here. Too many distractions. I need a quiet place. Somewhere–"

"Comfortable? Familiar?" she interjected.

Anna sighed. "Yeah, something like that."

"No better place than home."

"I suppose."

"*Then* what? After you finish the book, I mean."

"I'm not sure. Get a job until it gets published, I guess. I haven't thought that far ahead. *But* I won't be staying in Garrison. That much I know."

Claire sat in awe, still trying to process Anna's long-awaited homecoming "When will ya be here?"

"Friday. I have to pack and tie up some loose ends. Oh, and Claire, there's something else...more like a favor."

"Name it."

"I was hoping to stay at the cottage, if it's available."

"Shoot, that sign hasn't read *occupied* in years. Consider it yours."

"I'll pay you for it, of course."

"No, you won't! I ain't taking a dime. Having you here means more to me than money." She paused. "You're family."

"Thanks, Claire. I appreciate it. See you Friday."

"Friday it is."

Chapter Seven

Bryce floored the gas pedal. "What took so long?"

Jake swallowed a swig of beer. "I got out, didn't I?"

Bryce glared at him in the rearview mirror. His steel blue eyes squinted. His upper lip snarled. Jake took another gulp and stared out the window, regretting his choice of words.

Veering onto the I-190 expressway, Bryce merged into the right lane, guzzling what was left of his beer before tossing the amber bottle out the window. The faint sound of glass shattering on the highway could be heard as he kept driving.

"Next time, O'Connor, don't make me wait." With one hand draped over the steering wheel, he slouched down in the half-reclined seat. "Give me another beer."

Jake did what he was told. He always did what he was told when it came to Bryce.

He took a pack of cigarettes from his pocket, tapped the bottom with his palm, then pulled out a smoke. A smile tugged at the corners of his mouth as he moved the slender stick beneath his nose, inhaling the beautiful tobacco scent. Just holding the cigarette between his fingers put him at ease. With one easy movement, he slipped the pack back into his pocket and withdrew a black Zippo lighter. He flipped it open and lit the smoke, using his other hand as a windbreak. He sucked in a long drag and slowly exhaled.

As Jake watched the cloud of smoke dissipate, he thought back to his first attempt at smoking. He'd coughed and gagged, wondering how millions of people found enjoyment in such a gross habit. The odor repulsed him, and his mouth tasted like a fireplace filled with ashes. Just a few weak puffs had made him nauseous and dizzy, and he'd gasped for air, struggling to finish the cigarette right down to the butt.

Bryce held out his hand. "Give me one."

Again, Jake complied.

From the passenger seat, Jordan turned around and pulled out a cigarette from the pack. "Don't mind if I do."

Bryce sped down the fifty-five mile an hour expressway going seventy. The farther he drove, the less traffic there was.

Guiding the Mustang into the right lane, he took Exit 10, ran through the stop sign at the end of the short ramp, made an immediate left, followed by another sharp left onto the first street directly below the concrete overpass. Letting up on the gas, he pulled over and cut the engine.

Bryce and Jordan got out of the car. Jake slid across the black leather seat and took another swig from his beer bottle. He stepped out of the Mustang and stared at the dilapidated scene. He'd never been on that side of city but knew of its reputation. The run-down area surrounded a strip of deplorable, vacant homes used as meeting places for drug activity and temporary shelters for the homeless. One time thriving industrial buildings sat idle, their windows smashed out. An eerie sensation hovered over the neighborhood, especially at night.

Jake took another drag from his cigarette then asked, "What are we going to do?"

Bryce grabbed Jake's backpack, unzipped it, and pulled out a can of spray paint. "See that building," he said, cocking his head in the direction of a large brick structure.

"Yeah. What about it?"

Bryce shook the can of paint. "Looks like it needs a little color."

Bryce's cheeks caved inward as he took a deep drag from his cigarette. He stepped back, admiring his initials, BL, sprayed in red and outlined in black on the brick building facing the Niagara River. He nodded in satisfaction while exhaling the smoke.

Jordan had mimicked Bryce's idea from size and color to style and penmanship. But it was Jake's design that caught his attention.

"That's some fine artwork, O'Connor."

The Buffalo Sabres's logo in blue, gold, and white was smaller than his friends' initials, but the detailed work made up for its lack of size.

"I've seen better," Bryce said, bringing the cigarette up to his lips.

Every gang has a leader. The one who decides what to do, when to do it, and where to do it. The one who calls the shots. The one in charge. In Jake's very small gang, that leader was Bryce and had been since the day they'd met. A day he'd never forget.

Jake sighed with regret as he stared at the sign taped to the door that read DETENTION.

I wished I'd made it to class on time, then I wouldn't be stuck here.

He walked inside Room 105 to serve his hour-long sentence. During school, it was the Spanish room. After school, it had morphed into a jail cell.

He immediately noticed he was the first student there. Now he was punctual. Too little too late.

Jake sat down at a desk in the front row. His backpack fell to the floor with a thud.

Four colorful maps of Spain brought the white-walled room to life. One map detailed the entire country with major cities and small towns, while the other three geographical guides zoomed in on regions surrounding Madrid, Barcelona, and Cordoba.

The maps gave Jake something to stare at while he wondered if he was the only kid in the whole school to wind up in detention. Then the door swung open. He looked over to see Bryce standing next to Jordan. At six-foot-two, Bryce towered over his skinny sidekick. His wide shoulders and beefy biceps alone could've instantly landed him on the wrestling team.

Tales of the infamous Bryce Lindell had spread around school like an infectious disease. Most stories ended with an afterschool fight that left his victims with black eyes and bloody lips.

Careful not to draw attention to himself, Jake faced the blackboard. From the corner of his eye, he saw the bully's feet moving slowly toward him. Bryce stopped and slapped his meaty hands on the desk. Leaning over, his cigarette-tainted breath seeped from his mouth and lingered in Jake's face.

"Hey."

Jake gulped. "Me?" he asked, hoping not to get pummeled.

"Yeah, you. Who else you think I'm talking to?" He huffed. "Your name, what is it?"

"J-Jake...O'Connor."

"Well, O'Connor, I like to know what the newbies did to wind up in my home away from home." He leaned in closer, waiting for an answer.

"I...uh...was late to class."

"Beachman, right?" Bryce snorted. "That old bag."

"Yeah, that old bag." Jordan jerked his blond buzzed-cut head back as he laughed.

Cautiously, Jake asked, "What about you?"

Bryce sneered. "What about me, what?"

"I mean...umm...why are you guys here?"

Bryce stood straight up and folded his arms across his chest. "I tossed that loser Harold Simmons in the pool."

"I helped," Jordan chimed in, cackling.

Jake couldn't decipher if Bryce was trying to impress him or scare him.

He leaned over the desk again. "You're going to hang with us Saturday night."

Jake's eyes grew wide. "Umm, I'm not sure if can."

Bryce snarled. "That wasn't a question."

Jake glanced at Jordan.

"Yeah, man, you don't have a choice."

Jake was trapped. A refusal meant he'd be Bryce's next target. For his own safety, he agreed. "Okay. W-what are we going to do?"

"Don't worry," Bryce said with a grin that sent chills down Jake's spine. "I'll think of something."

Chapter Eight

After reading the same paragraph three times, Anna called it quits. She slammed the book shut and tossed it on her nightstand where it landed with a thud that echoed in her bedroom.

Reading before bed usually relaxed her enough to fall asleep, but not tonight. A bottle of sleeping pills couldn't knock her out.

Her impending trip to Garrison filled her mind with questions she didn't have the answers to. She was like a piece of metal being drawn to a magnet, unable to resist its pull. What was drawing her to Garrison? She had no idea. Nothing made sense. The more she pondered her decision, the more confusion clouded her thoughts. She felt trapped in a weird dream, fighting to wake up.

Anna went into the kitchen and flicked on the light switch. Four white canisters were lined up along the counter wall in descending order according to size. She opened the ceramic lid to the smallest canister marked *Tea* only to be disappointed. Not a single bag inside. "Great," she huffed, forcing the lid back on the canister.

The wall clock next to the refrigerator read 11:35. It was late, but another fifteen minutes wouldn't matter.

She grabbed her purse off the coffee table, pulled out her keys to lock the door, and left the apartment.

Bryce steered the Mustang toward the curb near the entrance of Allen's Corner Store. He stepped out of the sports car, followed by Jordan and Jake. They took a final drag from their cigarettes and flicked the smoldering butts onto the sidewalk.

As they walked into the store, a bell chimed. The store was empty except for a middle-aged man stacking bags of potato chips on a shelf near the coffee counter. He peeked his balding head out from behind the shelf and pursed his lips together at the sight of the teens. An irritated sigh escaped through his widening nostrils like a bull gearing up for an arena fight.

Bryce jerked his chin up, giving Jake and Jordan the signal to take their positions at the magazine racks while he swaggered toward the coolers in the back of the store.

Jake took a *Sports Illustrated* from the rack and thumbed through the magazine, looking up occasionally to see if the man had walked away from the shelf. He hadn't.

Jake became more restless with every flip of the page. He could feel the man's stare focused on him as if he was a hunter and Jake was his prey.

Bryce returned to the magazine rack and flashed open

his jacket just enough for Jake and Jordan to see the beer he swiped.

The bell chimed again as another customer entered the store. Jake waited a moment before walking down an aisle with toiletries at one end and canned goods at the other.

Once he arrived at the wall of coolers, he slowly unzipped his backpack, careful not to make a sound. He opened the glass door, grabbed the first large beer can he saw, and slipped it inside his bag.

He was halfway down the aisle on his way back to the magazine rack when he heard footsteps behind him. His heart raced and he broke out in a cold sweat. He was going to get caught. He couldn't get busted! He knew what would happen if he got arrested again. He had to see who was following him. The temptation was too great to resist. He couldn't wait another second. It had to be now.

In one swift motion, Jake turned around and came face to face with a strange woman.

Anna jumped back at the teen's unexpected move.

Fear cascaded across his thin face as his mousy brown hair fell over his eyes. He had a slim body frame hidden underneath a faded black T-shirt and oversized jeans. But it was his blue-stained fingers fumbling with his backpack strap that made her take notice.

"Excuse me," she said.

He stepped aside, and she took a box of green tea off the shelf. As she walked to the register at the front of the store, she looked back at him and that's when it hit her. *His eyes.* There was something about them that made her think she'd seen him before.

He joined two other teens huddled around the magazine rack as Anna approached the counter, waiting for the store owner to cash her out.

"Hi, Mr. Allen," she said, pulling out her wallet from her purse.

He held up the box and raised an eyebrow. "That's your second one this week, Anna."

"What can I say?" she said with a shrugged shoulder. "It's an addiction."

He scanned the code on the box. "Three twenty-five."

She handed him a five-dollar bill. The registered dinged when it opened, and he retrieved the change. "A dollar seventy-five," he said, placing the money in her hand.

His eyes shifted to the three loitering teens. He leaned over the edge, slammed his hands down on the counter, and barked, "Are you kids going to buy something or what?"

"Relax, pops," the tallest teen said.

"Don't call me pops, smart mouth. God help your real father."

"Just chill out, we're not done looking."

"This is mini mart, kid, not a mall."

The skinny blonde joined in. "We can't make up our minds. Your selection is so impressive," he said with a cackle.

Mr. Allen flew out from behind the counter, boldly waving his index finger. "Look, you punks, I've told you before, if you don't buy something, get out!"

Without a word, the tallest teen calmly pulled a handgun from the inside of his jacket as if he'd done it a dozen times and pointed the weapon at Mr. Allen's face.

"We're not ready to leave."

Anna's foot inched off the floor.

The gunman swung the weapon in her direction. "Don't move," he commanded.

Her fingers curled around the edge of the counter, gripping the white structure for support while her trembling body stood five feet from the barrel.

How ironic. She'd written up hundreds of robberies at Channel 3 News. They'd always seemed like fictional stories filled with drama and suspense. But the robberies were real, the people were real, and the fears were real. Standing there at gunpoint, she understood the sheer terror every store owner and patron who'd been robbed had felt.

"Your purse. Give it to me."

Anna's outstretched arm shook, and she dropped the sack. It made a thud sound when it hit the floor. A risky move, but she had to do something.

The gunman snorted. "You think I'll bend down, pick it

up, and you'll do some fancy kick move. Knock the gun out my hand? Is that it?"

She didn't answer him.

He shook his head. "What a stupid broad."

His remark made her furious, but she overlooked it. After all, there was a gun in his hand.

Glancing at the purse on the floor, then at Anna, he ordered her to pick it up.

She couldn't move.

His voice escalated. "Unless you want a bullet between those pretty little eyes, you better pick it up now!"

Bending down, her knees cracked. Her hands froze at her side but raised high enough where he could see them. The purse felt like there were bricks inside. She didn't take her eyes off the gun. Before she had the chance to fully stand up, he snatched the bag from her grasp.

He sneered and stepped toward her. Smiling, he looked Anna up and down, enjoying the view in front of him. His brawny hand wrapped around her face. He squeezed her cheeks in a sick way of showing sadistic affection. She flinched at his touch. She didn't know what scared her more, the gun in his hand or the way he stared at her like he wanted more than just the purse.

"Come on man, leave her alone."

The gunman turned around. "What did you say, O'Connor?"

"I...uh...um..."

"That's what I thought."

For whatever reason, he let go of Anna's face and aimed the gun at Mr. Allen's plump torso. "Open the register, pops."

The store owner clenched his mouth. He reached over the counter and pressed the open button on the register. The machine dinged, and the cash drawer popped out. He turned around and waited for his next instruction.

Glancing over his shoulder, the gunman barked out another order. "Get the cash, O'Connor."

He didn't move.

"What are you deaf or dumb? Move! Get the cash!"

The teen's slow walk to the counter looked like he was on his way to his execution. His mouth hung open as at the sight of the opened register drawer. His trembling hand reached for the money. The closer his fingers got to the cash, the more they shook. He looked at Anna, then at Mr. Allen, and finally the gunman. "I–I can't."

"Take the money!"

"I can't do it."

"O'Connor, if you don't get the cash, I will drop you right here, right now."

The skinny blonde sprinted behind the register and shoved O'Connor into the cigarette shelf, sending packages of Marlboro and Camels flying. He yanked the bills from the register. Confusion rippled across his face as he held a fistful of cash in the air. "There's only, like, fifty bucks here!"

The gunman stepped closer to Mr. Allen, pointing the

weapon an inch from his face. "Where's the rest of it?"

The stubborn store owner said nothing, just indignantly stared into his eyes.

"Come on man!" The skinny blonde screeched, jumping down from behind the counter. "Forget it. Let's bolt."

"Shut up! Just shut up!" The gunman cocked the revolver. "Where is it?"

Mr. Allen sighed and jerked his head in the direction of the counter. "Back there. In the safe."

"Open it."

The gunman wedged the weapon in Mr. Allen's back, marching his victim to the safe. But the store owner swung around in a daring attempt to grab the gun. The beer bottle fell out of the gunman's jacket and smashed into tiny pieces. The struggle sent them tumbling to the concrete floor.

Both sets of hands gripped the gun, fighting for possession when a noise that sounded like a car backfiring erupted.

But it wasn't a car.

A bullet sailed through the front window where it fractured the glass like a spider web. Anna screamed and threw her hands over her head as she hit the ground. The gunman scrambled to his feet and toppled a display of packaged donuts and pastries onto Mr. Allen, burying him in boxes before fleeing the store with the skinny blonde right behind him.

Anna crawled over to the store owner where he lay next

to a puddle of blood. "Mr. Allen, your hand!"

A shard of glass had left a nasty gash in his palm, but that didn't stop him from getting up.

Just as he made it to his feet, the teen behind the counter ran out of the store.

Mr. Allen and Anna went after him, but he was already too far down the block to catch him on foot.

In the distance, a police car was coming toward the store. Darting out into the street, Mr. Allen wildly waved his blood drenched hand and shouted, "I just got robbed!" He pointed to the small figure sprinting down Forest Avenue.

The police officer hit the gas and sped down the road with the red and blue lights flashing and siren blaring.

Chapter Nine

Jake ducked down an alley not big enough for even the smallest car. Behind him, a voice called out, "Hey you! Stop!"

There was a chain link fence at the end of the alley. Jake catapulted himself midway up the metal links and scrambled to the top, heaved himself over the other side, and plunged to the ground.

His body ached from the impact of the ten-foot fall. The top layer of skin on his palms was gone. His hands stung from the exposed flesh. His legs couldn't run another five feet. But he needed a place to hide, so he dashed behind a dumpster, camouflaging himself next to the metal box and evening darkness.

The sound of footsteps became louder.

Jake pressed himself closer to the corner where the edge of the dumpster met a brick wall as he watched the officer run past his hiding spot.

He gasped for air. Sinking down into a squatting position, he wished he was back at the house. Sitting on the couch watching *NCIS* with the others sounded good. Even being locked in his messy room and lying on his unmade bed with nothing to do was better than hiding behind a foul-smelling dumpster trying to escape the police for a robbery he technically didn't commit.

Mr. Allen's wounded hand flashed before him. The cut had looked painful, and he'd been bleeding a lot.

What if I run into Mr. Allen? What if that woman gives a description to the police?

One "what if" after another raced through Jake's mind. His hands began to shake. He needed a smoke. He pulled out his cigarettes and stared at the crushed pack. Luckily, none of them were broken in half.

What if they catch me? Maybe not tonight but tomorrow? Or the next day or next week?

He thought about living in fear, afraid to walk down the street. Wondering if he was being watched. His hand trembled as he pulled out a cigarette. Then he realized his backpack was gone.

He remembered the sack thumping against his back when he was running. He stopped to scan the five-foot radius around him and saw it lying near the fence. It must have fallen off his shoulders when he hit the ground.

Jake crept away from his hiding spot. The cops were gone. He was all alone in the alley. Retrieving the backpack would be easy. All he had to do was get the bag and go home—a three-mile walk he wasn't thrilled about.

He needed an alternative route. Side streets and cutting through properties was the quickest way back to the house. Quickly, he devised a plan as he jogged out from behind the dumpster and swooped down to pick up the bag.

Go down the alley, get on Miller Street, cut over on Vermont to Rounds...

A pair of hands grabbed him from behind. Jake wrestled to break free from the officer's tight grip. In one swift move, he forced him to the ground.

"Dumb move, kid. You have the right to remain silent," he said, taking a pair of handcuffs from his belt. He clicked the first cuff around Jake's wrist. He winced as the metal pinched his skin. "If you give up that right, anything you say can and will be used against you."

The officer clicked the second cuff shut and finished reading him his rights.

Chapter Ten

The dim lighting and cement floor at the police station reminded Anna of a primetime cop show. The wooden bench creaked every time she crossed and uncrossed her legs.

A steady stream of incoming calls kept a female officer busy while she thumbed through a magazine. Occasionally, an officer walked through the waiting area. Anna recognized a few of the law enforcers who had been interviewed by Channel 3 News reporters. They looked different in person.

She expected to see a suspect's fervent attempt to break free from the grip of two officers while screaming, "I didn't do it. You got the wrong guy!" She imagined voices escalating between detectives and cops after a botched attempt to capture the bad guy.

But those scenarios belonged on television. This was real life. She was in a real police station with real criminals. A shiver ran through her body thinking about the drug addicts, murderers, and thieves past the door in the holding center.

She glanced at the clock hanging on the wall. It was twelve forty-five in the morning.

Resting her head against the cement block wall, she fought to keep her eyes open when a familiar voice pulled her out of a sleepy state. She craned her neck and peeked down the hallway. An officer escorted Mr. Allen to the exit. His white uniform dress shirt—opposed to the standard blue uniform shirt—indicated a higher rank.

"Thanks again for coming down, Mr. Allen." The officer pointed to the store owner's wound. "You really should get that checked out."

The store owner glanced at the bloody rag wrapped around his hand. "I'll be fine. I may be an old man to some punks, but a few cuts aren't going hurt me," he said with a huff.

A gentle smile eased across the officer's face. "I know, but please have a doctor take a look at it. Okay?"

"Yeah, yeah." Mr. Allen waved his hand, brushing off the injury as if it were nothing. "I'll tell you what would really make me feel better. Catching those hoods and locking them up. That's what I want."

Anna stood up, eager to hear more of their conversation. She grabbed her purse and walked toward the two men. The squeak from the battered bench echoed.

A red hue surfaced in Mr. Allen's cheeks. "Well, at least you got one of 'em behind bars. I didn't work hard my whole life to let some no-good rotten kids take me out and take what belongs to me." He pointed his thumb at his chest. "That's for sure."

"I understand how you feel, Mr. Allen. We'll do everything we can to help. Now, why don't you head over to the emergency room and get that hand checked out?" The officer held the door open and patted the store owner's shoulder. "We'll be in touch as soon as anything new develops."

Anna opened her mouth, but Mr. Allen left before she had a chance to call out his name. Then a teenager, not much older than the ones she'd seen at the store, walked past her in handcuffs.

"Sit here," the officer with him ordered.

Clad in a white sleeveless T-shirt and torn jeans, the young man plopped down on a plastic chair. Tattoos covered his exposed arms and his disheveled facial hair needed to be introduced to a sharp razor. He slouched against the concrete wall while the officer conversed with the officer at the desk.

Anna clutched her purse close to her chest.

As if he felt her stare, he angled his head toward her. A cocky grin spread across his face. "Hey, baby, you are one fine lookin' woman."

"Get up!" The officer grabbed the suspect's arm and yanked him to his feet. "And get moving."

"Come back and visit me." His lips puckered up, blowing Anna a kiss.

The gesture made her nose crinkle in disgust like she'd swallowed spoiled milk.

Mr. Allen was gone, and she'd given her statement about the robbery. There was no reason for her to hang around a depressing police station, except one.

Anna couldn't stop thinking about the teen locked in a cell. His face was etched in her brain. She recognized him, but why? From where? She thought about places she had been—not that the list was very long. She pictured acquaintances, trying to piece together any information.

Nothing.

The more Anna thought about him, the more tired she became. She longed for her bed and a good night's sleep. She made a mental note to go to the convenience store the next afternoon to check on Mr. Allen.

Walking to the exit, she slung her purse over her shoulder and was nearly knocked over when a dark-haired woman stormed into the police station. She marched to the front desk where the female officer was so engrossed in her magazine, she didn't notice her hovering over the desk.

The woman let out an agitated sigh that could be heard across the room. "Excuse me," she said, fearlessly tilting the magazine down with one finger. "I'm Stephanie Grey. I'm here for Jake O'Connor."

The officer peered up and tugged the magazine from the rude woman's grasp. "What did you say the name was?"

"Jake O'Connor. O apostrophe C-O-N-" Stephanie said, slowly spelling as if she were speaking to child.

The officer raised her hand, signaling for her to stop. "No

need for that, Ma'am." She pushed backed her chair. It came to a rolling stop at a four-tiered metal filing cabinet. After opening the drawer labeled *O - T*, she thumbed through the Os, reading each file out loud.

"Oates, Odes, O'Connelly, here it is, O'Connor." She pulled the file out and returned to the desk. With her glasses resting on the midsection of her nose, she quickly scanned the report. "Oh yeah, the Allen store robbery." She raised her eyebrows. "Kinda young wouldn't you say?"

The officer's smirk added fuel to Stephanie's already raging fire. "How much is bail?"

"For armed robbery? Probably about fifty grand."

Stephanie huffed, shaking her head.

Anna went toward the desk, hoping to learn more about the incarcerated teen when the officer who had been with Mr. Allen moments earlier came around the corner.

"Ms. Grey?" he questioned.

"Yes."

"I'm Lieutenant Dean Macalister." The pleasant officer extended his hand. "Thanks for coming down so late."

Stephanie adjusted her purse strap, hiking up the leather band on her shoulder as she received his handshake. "Is Jake okay?"

"Physically, yes." The lieutenant's hands landed on his hips. "Legally...that's another story."

"Excuse me?" Anna said.

The officer turned and gave her a questioning look.

71

"I'm Anna Sutton. I was at the store tonight when–"

"Oh, yes, Miss Sutton. Did you give your statement?"

"Yes, I did."

"Thanks, we appreciate it. You can go home now."

But Anna wasn't ready to leave. Something wasn't right. Who was this woman? Her last name was Grey, and Jake's was O'Connor. Maybe she remarried? Stepmom perhaps?

"Are you Jake's mom?" she asked.

The woman grunted. "Mom? No, I'm his social worker."

"Social worker?" Anna whispered in confusion.

The lieutenant stared at her as she tried to make the connection. "Ladies, let's go to my office where we can talk privately."

Lieutenant Macalister led them down a short hallway. He opened the door to his office and motioned with his hand for them to take a seat. He shut the door, sat down, and let out a sigh as he leaned forward on his desk, hands clasped together.

"Miss Sutton, Jake's father, David, was a member on our force." The lieutenant hesitated, tapping the tips of his fingers. "He was a great guy and a great friend, not to mention one heck of an officer. He loved being a cop. It was an honor for him to wear his uniform. This wasn't just his job. David felt it was his reason for living. To make a difference."

The officer cleared his throat before continuing.

"Seven years ago, David pulled over a driver for

speeding. A routine traffic stop, nothing out of the ordinary, until he approached the driver. Turns out, he was a fugitive. The man shot David."

Anna leaned forward. "Wait a minute. Did you say seven years ago?"

Lieutenant Macalister sighed. "Yes. September to be exact."

"I remember that. I was working at Channel 3 News, and the scanners went crazy about an officer being shot. We broke in during programming every hour with updates and new information. At midnight...he died."

The lieutenant looked as if he was reliving the horror of that night all over again.

Suddenly, Anna knew where she'd seen Jake.

"The funeral!" she blurted out. "That's how I know Jake. His father's funeral. The station naturally covered it," she said, replaying the story in her head. "He stood next to the casket wearing a dark suit. But he wasn't crying. Not a single tear."

The stoic expression on Jake's face was unforgettable. Watching the video in the control room, Anna had found herself grieving for him. She understood his pain even though they'd never met.

"What about his mom? Where's she?"

Stephanie interjected. "Faye O'Connor died two years ago from breast cancer. She didn't have a will so there wasn't a legal guardian named for Jake to live with. The closest relative is his grandmother, but she's in a nursing home with Alzheimer's. He has a few great aunts and second cousins, but they all had excuses why they couldn't take him in."

"Who's taking care of him now?" Anna asked.

"He's a ward of the state. He's been with a handful of foster families but messed up every chance to get adopted. For the last six months, he's been living at a short-term group home for kids waiting to be adopted or put into foster care." With an annoyed huff she added, "And troubled kids like Jake."

Anna turned her attention to the lieutenant. "What's going to happen to him now?"

"He's a minor, so he'll probably wind up in Wyatt Hall until he turns eighteen."

"Isn't that a detention center for kids?"

Stephanie quickly corrected her. "We call them long-term facilities. Kids who end up at Wyatt are violent, have major drug problems, some are suicidal, and they all have an arrest record." She folded her arms and grunted. "Once you go to Wyatt, there isn't a family out there that's going to want you."

"I know it sounds better than jail, Miss Sutton," Lieutenant Macalister said, "but believe me, if I had to choose between Wyatt or jail, I'd choose jail."

His discouraging words made Anna feel worse.

"But he's just a kid without a family. That's not his fault."

"Just because his parents are dead doesn't give him a pass to break the law," Stephanie shouted. "Do I feel bad for Jake? Yes, of course I do. But he's gotta be accountable for his actions. Let me ask you something, Miss Sutton. How did you feel tonight at the store? You were scared? Terrified? I'm sure you wondered if you were going to make it out alive. Right?"

Anna subtly rolled her eyes as if the answer was obvious. "Yeah, so?"

"So that's what the next person will feel, and the next one, and the one after that."

"Do you really care about what happens to Jake, or are you just trying to dump him off on someone else? One less file for you to deal with, hmm, Ms. Grey?"

Stephanie's dark brown eyes squinted. "I take offense to that remark."

"Good," Anna shouted back. "It was meant to be offensive."

"I look after these kids. I'm the one trying to place them with good families. I'm the only person they've got!"

"That doesn't say a whole lot."

"How dare you!" Stephanie growled. "Who do you think you are coming in here–"

Lieutenant Macalister jumped from his chair. "Ladies, ladies please!" His arms spread wide like a referee. "We're getting off track. Calm down. Both of you." He sat back down.

Stephanie crossed her arms and huffed. "Miss Sutton, you don't understand what kind of kid we're talking about here. Jake breaks curfew, he drinks, he smokes. He's been caught stealing stuff at the home. And," she added smugly, "this isn't his first arrest. The last family called the cops after he took a swing at the foster father because the man asked him to take out the trash. *The trash!* Jake denied it, of course, but the wife backed up her husband. And these *friends* he's hanging around are dangerous. Tonight, case in point."

Lieutenant Macalister looked at Anna with his kind blue eyes. "Miss Sutton, I understand you feel badly for Jake," he said with equal empathy, "but Ms. Grey is right. Jake needs to take responsibility for his actions. My officers are bringing in kids like him three, four times a week. They're running rampant, causing all kinds of trouble. Stealing and destroying property. As a matter of fact, a short time after the robbery, we got an anonymous call from a man who said he saw a bunch of kids down by the river spray painting graffiti on the old Edmonton building. I have a hunch it was Jake and his buddies."

That explains the blue paint on his fingers.

"People are afraid to leave their homes and walk down the streets in that neighborhood. Look, I'm sure there's good in Jake. There has to be, he's David's son. But if he doesn't learn now, I'm afraid one day he's going to be the one pulling the trigger.

Anna wasn't getting anywhere. She knew when she was outnumbered. She thanked the officer for his time and left the police station.

She returned to the comfort of her apartment, unlike Jake who was locked away in a cold jail cell. He had to be afraid. What kid wouldn't be in that situation? As much as it pained her to admit, Lieutenant Macalister was right. Jake was headed down a dangerous road and there wasn't a thing anyone could do for him, including her.

But she had to see him one more time.

Chapter Eleven

From the back row of the courtroom, Anna watched a stenographer enter the room through a side entrance. The woman checked the roll of paper in her machine then left through the same side entrance.

Anna balanced her elbow on the arm of the chair while her head rested in her hand. Her eyelids drooped, fighting to stay open. Eventually she gave in and snuck a few winks of sleep before Jake's arraignment.

She'd expected to sleep like a rock after getting home from the police station. Not the case. Flopping around in bed like a flounder washed up on the shore, thoughts of Jake, the robbery, and Garrison consumed her. When she had finally drifted off, the morning sunrays poked through the plastic blinds making it impossible for her to fall back asleep.

Anna's conversation with Lieutenant Macalister and Stephanie Grey weighed heavy on her mind. To lose a parent at any age was tough, but Jake had gone through it twice. Without warning, his family had been ripped away from him. It wasn't fair. Sadly, she could relate.

The echo of a door shutting interrupted her thoughts when the stenographer came back in carrying a large roll of paper. She was feeding it into the machine when a tall man in a black suit entered from the back and walked down the aisle. He dropped his briefcase onto the table, opened the case, and pulled out a manila folder.

Anna stood up and tugged at the bottom of her shirt to smooth out any wrinkles. Slowly, she walked to the front of the courtroom where he perused the file in his hand.

She cleared her throat. "Excuse me, are you Jake O'Connor's lawyer?"

No response.

Speak up, Anna.

She cleared her throat again. "Are you Jake O'Connor's lawyer?" she asked, elevating her voice as she peered up at him.

Turning his head just enough to look at her from the corner of his eye, he sighed. Reaching inside his suit jacket, he pulled out a pair of Ray-Ban glasses and fumbled with them before putting them on. He glanced at the name on the folder. "It appears that way." He shoved the glasses back in his suit pocket and tossed the folder on the table. "Robert Finny, public defender. And you are?"

"Anna Sutton. I was at Allen's Corner Store last night."

Pouring a glass of water from the pitcher on the table, the lawyer remained standing with his back to her. He took his time drinking the water.

The deafening silence made Anna snap like a brittle branch.

"He didn't do it!"

Robert choked on the drink. He coughed and pounded a clenched fist to his chest as he gasped for air. Finally, he turned around with his lips partially separated in awe. "Did I hear you right? You said he didn't do it?"

Suddenly, Anna felt very small, like a naughty kid about to get a tongue lashing for swearing.

"You think armed robbery is nothing? Last time I looked that one up in my law books, it was listed under the crime category."

The lawyer's belittling tone made her want to curl up in the corner and hide. She had to clarify her explanation.

"I meant Jake wasn't the one with the gun."

"It doesn't matter."

"Well, it should."

"He was a willing participant."

Anna let out an absurd snort. "No, he wasn't. He didn't know about the gun or the robbery."

"Oh really?" Robert said with a feigned puzzled look. "And how would *you* know that? What are you, psychic or something?"

She fired back, "I could tell."

"That's solid evidence, Miss Sutton. I'll be sure to use that one."

"I saw the look on his face."

Robert bellowed a "Ha!" shaking his head as he slammed the lid to his briefcase shut.

"What's so funny?"

"In case you forgot, you're an eyewitness to the crime. The prosecution's case is airtight."

"That's right! I was there," Anna shouted, pointing her finger at him. *"You* weren't." *Shut up, Anna. Just shut up. You're making it worse.* "He didn't know his friends were going to rob the store."

"Sure, the judge will take your word for it. Then he'll drop the charges, set the delinquent free, and you'll be the hero of the day."

Her blood boiled at his condescending tone.

"Or maybe Mr. O'Connelly should've picked some better friends to hang with. Then he wouldn't be in this mess."

"It's O'Connor," Anna said. "Jake O'Connor."

"Whatever. This is how it's going to work. Mr. *O'Connor,"* he emphasized, "is going to plead guilty, spend time in juvey, and hopefully not see the inside of another jail for a long time." His voice trailed off. "Although I doubt it."

Anna's nostrils flared. "Aren't you going to even try to get the charges dropped or reduced or something? You are his defense lawyer. That's your job."

"This is an open and shut case. I'm sure Mr. Allen won't hesitate to take the stand. Look, if O'Connor pleads not guilty that means a trial. Then what happens is the taxpayers' money gets wasted. But more importantly," he said, bringing his hand to his chest, "my time gets wasted."

During Anna's squabble with Robert Finny, the bailiff

81

had entered the courtroom. Jake's arraignment was ready to begin. He was the reason she was there, not to get in a playground argument with his arrogant lawyer.

As she turned around to go back to her seat, she stopped halfway down the aisle when she saw Stephanie. The social worker gave a smug glare as she sat down. Anna didn't have to guess whose side she was on. She continued to her seat and sat down.

The court stenographer adjusted her skirt and took her position at her machine. The bailiff stood next to the bench as the door behind him opened with a squeak.

Jake emerged wearing the same pair of baggy jeans and faded black T-shirt he'd worn the night before. An officer escorted him to the defense table. The teen's drooped head prevented him from making eye contact with anyone in the room as he stood next to the lawyer.

Looking at Robert, Anna couldn't hold back a disgusted snort. *The kid has a better shot representing himself.*

The bailiff announced the judge's entrance with an authoritative, "All rise."

Stephanie and Anna remained standing as the judge made his way behind the bench. The bailiff called out, "Case number 859276. The State of New York versus Jacob O'Connor, the honorable Judge Henry Roland presiding."

Anna gasped as her fingers hovered over her lips. *"Henry?"*

The judge took Jake's file from the bailiff. "Be seated," he said, addressing the audience. He put on his wire-rimmed glasses, opened the file, and perused the charges. He uttered a "huh" and a few "hmms" under his breath as he flipped to the next page.

The judge held up the file in his hand and locked his eyes on Jake, who slouched in his seat. "Mr. O'Connor, this is quite a list. Do you realize the gravity of these charges?"

The teen barely nodded.

An aggravated huff seeped past Judge Roland's lips as he shook his head. "Mr. Finny, how does your client plead?"

The lawyer stood up, his chin pointed out. "Guilty, your honor."

"Mr. O'Connor, please stand."

Robert nudged Jake for him to get up.

"Jacob O'Connor, I hereby sentence you to Wyatt Hall effective immediately. You will remain in the facility until you turn eighteen years of age and be on probation for the next five years. In addition, I order you to two years of community service. That is all. Case dismissed."

With the gavel poised in midair ready to be slammed down, Anna felt an urge to intervene. She didn't have a speech prepared. A nervous energy forced her to her feet. Suddenly, she heard the words "Your Honor?" come blazing out of her mouth.

Without looking up he replied, "What is it?"

"Is there anything else that can be done for this young man?"

That got his attention. Immediately, his head shot up. The judge removed his glasses and squinted in bewilderment when he recognized Anna.

Jake whipped his head around.

"Before we adjourn, I'd like to see Mr. Finny and the young lady in my chambers." He hit his gavel, whispered something to the bailiff—who nodded his head—and then left the courtroom.

The court officer motioned with his hand for Robert and Anna to come forward. "This way please," he said.

Anna didn't know what Henry was up to, but she had a feeling their reunion wasn't going to be spent catching up on old times.

Chapter Twelve

Robert and Anna followed the bailiff as he escorted them inside the judge's chambers where Henry came out from behind his desk, heading straight for Anna.

"I can't believe it. Anna!" He bent over, giving her a hug.

She received his embrace and smiled. She'd forgotten how tall he was.

His hands landed on her shoulders. "It's been a long time."

Anna nodded in agreement. "Two years."

He led her to a crimson leather couch with brass buttons where he motioned for her to sit down. His picturesque chambers boasted vintage décor from paintings to table-top knickknacks. Hundreds of law books took up space on the dark wooden shelves. Framed photographs of his family sat poised on a large desk next to stacks of paperwork and two opened law books.

"How are things at the station?" he asked, unzipping his robe, revealing a white dress shirt and gray pants.

"Funny you ask. I quit a few weeks ago."

He looked concerned. "Anything wrong?"

"No, nothing like that. It was time for me to write my book. I've put it off long enough."

"Good for you." He hung the robe in the closet and shut the door "It's about time your name makes the bestseller's list."

"I suppose," she said with a chuckle. "I'm heading to Garrison for a few months. Less interruptions. Quiet...you know."

Aside from a few wrinkles around his blue eyes, Judge Henry Roland looked the same as the last time she'd seen him. Athletic. Fit. Strong. His slender build and thick, silver hair said distinguished, not old.

"Are you still running?" Anna asked as he sat down next to her while Robert stood in the middle of the room, gawking at them.

"Four times a week, like always. And it's going stay that way until my knees give out and my joints ache at the very thought of putting on my Saucony's."

Anna smiled. Same old Henry.

"What about you?"

"I make it outside when I can." She dipped her head in embarrassment. "Not as much since I left Channel 3."

Henry's love for running had inspired her to hit the pavement. At first, she'd hated it. She didn't think she'd make it a mile without stopping to catch her breath. After a few weeks, the dreaded exercise went beyond endurance and became something more. She felt at peace running during the early morning, feeling the light breeze hit her face. Watching the bright orange sun come up past the horizon. Hearing birds chirping as they hunted for breakfast. Running cleared her head. It started her day on a good note. She felt optimistic, eager to discover something new and exciting.

Engrossed in conversation with Henry, they forgot about Robert until he butted in. "Excuse me?" The furrow in his forehead sunk deeper. "How do you know each other?"

Henry and Anna chuckled. They hadn't purposely left the public defender out of the loop.

"I used to date his son." Turning to face the judge she asked, "How is Kyle, by the way?"

Henry slapped his palms on his thighs. "The same. Goes from job to job. No goals or direction. He tells me, 'Dad, relax, it's cool. I'm still trying to find my niche.' He's twenty-eight years old and still doesn't know what the word commitment means."

Like two buddies talking sports, Henry turned to Robert. "You know, when Kyle dated Anna, I told my wife, this is it." He pointed at Anna and smiled. "This is the one who will turn our boy around. But Anna, being an intelligent woman, saw that Kyle wasn't going to change. She knew there was no future for them. Come to think of it, I cried more than he did when she dumped him."

Anna could have spent the next few minutes reminiscing with the judge, but the time had come to address Jake and the robbery.

"Your Honor?"

"Anna, we're in my chambers. Call me Henry."

"Okay. Henry."

He patted her hand. "That's better."

"Jake made a mistake—a big mistake. He wasn't thinking, he knows that. But if you can just give him a second chance, I'm—"

"Can't," Henry said abruptly. "If I do, he'll end up back in my courtroom. Kids like him always do." He brought his hands together and rested his elbows on his knees. "How do you know Jake?"

"I don't. Well, not really. I just..."

"Just what?"

Anna shrugged her shoulders. "I feel bad for him."

Appalled at her response, Robert spewed out in disgust, "Feel bad for *him?* How about feeling bad for the poor old guy who owns the store, not the punk who held it up."

Anna stood up. "He's not a punk."

In less than thirty minutes, she found herself in a second shouting match with the lawyer.

"Oh, really? And how do you know that, Miss Sutton? You said it yourself you don't even know him."

"Both of his parents are dead. No one cares about him. Does it really surprise you he did what he did?" She glared at the public defender. "Jake is all alone. He probably thinks he's better off having friends like those jerks then having no one at all."

Henry leaned back in the leather couch, crossing one leg

over the other. "Anna, I get what you're saying, and you're right. To a point."

She sat back down, giving him her full attention.

"But if I let Jake off with a slap on the wrist, I guarantee the first thing he'll do is find his friends and pick up where they left off."

"But what if he doesn't?" she asked.

"Then they'll find him and lure him back. He's not strong enough to resist them. This isn't a game. He needs to learn his lesson."

Robert gently tugged at the French cuffs on his shirt. "I agree, Your Honor."

Anna rolled her eyes.

Henry looked up at the lawyer. "I didn't ask for your opinion."

When Anna walked into Henry's chambers, she'd convinced herself things would work out in Jake's favor, not because of her relationship with the judge but because she knew he was a good man. Strict but fair. Someone who believed in second chances. Now she wasn't sure. Her effort, as small as it was, got Jake nowhere.

"Sounds like your mind is made up." Her defeated tone sounded worse out loud.

Henry's half-hearted smile confirmed what they both already knew.

"I guess there's nothing left to say."

He patted her arm. "Guess not."

"Too bad. I wish I could help Jake."

Henry's brow furrowed. "What did you say?"

"I said I wish someone could help Jake."

He sat up, pointing his index finger. "No, you said, '*I...I wish I could help Jake.*'"

Casually, Anna corrected her error. "I misspoke. I meant someone else, not me."

Henry's eyebrow rose up. "Maybe there is someone who can help." A grin stretched across his face. She didn't like the way he was looking at her.

"Who?" she questioned. She hoped she was wrong. She hoped she was reading too much into his expression.

"How long are you going to be in Garrison?"

Anna shook her head before she answered. "I know what you're thinking, Henry. The answer is no."

"You're just the kind of person Jake needs."

"I misspoke." Her voice escalated and cracked. "I wasn't talking about me."

He cocked his head. "I think you were."

"No. Absolutely not. Jake cannot come with me to Indiana."

Robert jumped back into the conversation. "I'm with Miss Sutton."

Finally, she and the jerk lawyer found common ground.

Henry peered up. "Once again your opinion is irrelevant."

"I don't know the first thing about teenagers," Anna said.

"You were one, right?"

"What about the charges? What about Mr. Allen?"

Leaning back, he casually crossed his legs. "I can talk to George. We go way back. I'm sure we can work something out, given the new arrangement."

Sweat pooled in Anna's hands. "There is no new arrangement!"

But Henry just stared at her and smiled.

"I would be responsible for him."

"That's the point. He'll be in a nice rural setting far away from his friends. Who knows, maybe that Midwest goodness will rub off on him," he said with a wink.

"Jake doesn't even know me. I'm a stranger to him."

The judge clapped his hands together as if she'd finally understood an algebra problem. "Exactly! His expectations won't be high. Think about it, Anna. Everyone he knows has let him down. He's got nothing to lose with you."

She fidgeted with her fingers, fearfully mulling what could go wrong if she brought Jake with her to Garrison. "What if this turns out to be a disaster? What if–"

"Hey, I haven't been on the bench this long for being wrong."

Anna's meddling had come back to bite her. She wished she'd kept her mouth shut. Finishing her book was top priority. Returning to Garrison was about her, not being a role model to a troubled teen.

Then it happened. The ultimatum. Henry's countenance reverted back to serious. "Anna, it's this or Wyatt."

Chapter Thirteen

Anna was tucking the last suitcase into the trunk of her Jeep when she heard the door to the apartment building shut. She looked up to see Mrs. Elardo carefully walking down the brick steps holding a large brown paper bag.

She shut the trunk and met the landlord at the foot of the steps, eyeing up the grocery bag with the word "Wegmans" written across the middle.

"Hello, dear. I wanted to say goodbye and give you this." Mrs. Elardo handed her the sack for inspection. The heaviness spiked Anna's curiosity, but before she had a chance to peek inside, the old woman proudly listed the food items.

"Let's see, there's fresh fruit—apples, bananas, and grapes—homemade chocolate chip cookies," she used her fingers to count off the items, "a jug of lemonade, potato chips, and some big turkey sandwiches. I thought this would be much better than going to one of those dirty rest stops for a bucket of grease." She gently touched Anna's arm. "You need your strength to drive all that way."

Anna chuckled at the analogy, even though she was right. "Thank you, Mrs. Elardo. That was very sweet of you."

Her hand waved in front of her face. "Oh, it was nothing. I enjoyed doing it." She sighed. "I don't have many people to cook for these days." Her words trailed off and a layer of watery glaze coated her hazel eyes as she stared at the cracked sidewalk.

Mrs. Elardo was truly a sad sight.

Without a word, Anna walked to the Jeep and placed the bagged lunch on the floor of the back seat. Perhaps another expression of gratitude would make the old woman feel appreciated?

She returned to the curb and said, "Thanks again for getting my mail while I'm gone. And of course, the food. I can't wait to dig in."

Mrs. Elardo forced a smile.

"Oh, I almost forgot." Anna pulled a check from her pocket. "Here's three months' rent."

"Thank you, dear." She shoved the folded piece of paper into the pocket of her floral housecoat as a silver Honda Civic pulled up to the curb.

Anna glanced at her watch. Nine o'clock. Right on time.

Both women watched and waited for the driver and passenger to get out of the car. Finally, Stephanie emerged from the vehicle.

"Good morning," Anna said.

The social worker ignored the greeting and returned to the car. She tapped the window with the knuckle of her index finger. The single knock was Jake's cue to get out.

93

Bringing Jake to Garrison had meant Anna postponing the trip two weeks. After much persuasion from Henry, Mr. Allen conceded to the arrangement. The felony charges were bumped down to a misdemeanor with probation and community service as part of the teen's sentence.

The court granted her emergency foster care but getting clearance to take Jake across state lines proved to be the most challenging. After a lot of paperwork, and a lot of phone calls, Anna was authorized to take him out of New York. The crash course in emergency foster care policies and procedures did little to boost her confidence. Henry was the only one who had faith in her, while Stephanie was against the arrangement from conception. The phrase "crazy idea" must have come out of her mouth a thousand times.

As the social worker approached the curb, she nodded her head at Anna and shot an inquisitive look at Mrs. Elardo before bellowing out, "Hello."

The old woman smiled weakly, then flashed Anna a look of pity.

Anna watched from the side of the road as Jake sank lower in the back seat, leaving only the top of his head visible.

With a huff, Stephanie marched back to the vehicle like an angry drill sergeant and whipped open the passenger door. "Get out!"

He slid across the seat and slammed the car door.

Dragging his feet against the pavement, he hoisted his backpack over his shoulder. Stephanie followed him carrying a suitcase.

Anna took a deep breath. *You can do this.*

She stuck out her hand then pulled it back. Teens don't shake hands. A high-five would be ridiculous. Instead, she simply said, "Hi, Jake."

He looked away. No response. Not surprising.

"Got everything you need?" she asked.

His mouth formed a scowl.

"Here," Stephanie said, handing Anna the suitcase. The faded blue material made it look like something from the 1980s.

She held up the luggage. "This is it? You do know we're going be gone for two and a half months."

Stephanie huffed. "Yes, Anna, I'm well aware how long he'll be gone." She hiked her falling purse strap up on her shoulder. "I could barely get him to pack anything."

What have I gotten myself into?

Stephanie looked at Jake. "Come on. Time to go."

He didn't move.

She sighed, placing her hands on her hips. "I said, it's time to go."

"I can't believe you're making me do this," he shouted.

"Don't blame me. You did this to yourself."

He threw his body against the Jeep and pouted.

"Would it kill you to show a little bit of gratitude? You're

95

not in a maximum security detention hall thanks to her." Stephanie pointed to Anna like a ragged piece of furniture she'd found on the side of the road.

Don't you mean long-term facility, Ms. Grey? Oh, how Anna wanted to throw that in her face just as she'd done in Lieutenant Macalister's office. But she held her tongue.

"The kids in that place make your buddies look like naughty toddlers who need a timeout. Now, come on. Anna's waiting." She put her hand on his shoulder and forced him to walk.

He shuffled past Anna. She reached for his backpack and offered to put it in the trunk with the other luggage.

He swiped her hand away. "I got it!" He picked up the pace, got into the Jeep, and slammed the door.

Anna stared at Stephanie for help.

A crooked smile spread across the social worker's face. "Welcome to my world."

If Jake's outburst was any indication how the next ten hours on the road would be spent, not to mention the summer, she'd definitely bitten off more than she could chew. Maybe a few years locked up at Wyatt was the better alternative? Too late now.

Anna got in the Jeep and started the engine. Jake slouched in the front seat staring out the window. As she pulled away, she glanced in the rearview mirror watching the images of Stephanie and Mrs. Elardo become smaller until they were out of sight.

Chapter Fourteen

Driving in silence for four hours gave Anna plenty of time to think. She debated about different topics to broach, hoping to ignite a small conversation with Jake. One-word answers would suffice. But every time she opened her mouth, she stopped.

The quietness was uncomfortable but not unbearable. At least the weather cooperated with her travel plans. She couldn't have asked for a better forecast. Blue skies, seventy-five degrees, and nothing but sunshine.

They were ten miles shy of Cleveland when they passed a blue and white highway sign indicating a rest stop a mile up ahead. It was a good spot to take a break.

Anna pulled into the parking lot where a handful of wooden picnic benches on a grassy patch of land surrounded a convenience store and several gas pumps. A few semi-trucks were parked off to the side.

She parked the Jeep, anxious to get out and stretch her stiff legs. She grabbed Mrs. Elardo's bag of goodies from the back seat. "How about we have lunch? There's plenty."

Jake ignored her, staring out the window.

"Are you hungry? Do you want to eat?" she asked, hoping for a response.

Nothing.

She opened the door. "Fine. I'm going to sit at the picnic table. You're welcome to join me if you change your mind."

She left the Jeep and walked to a nearby bench. She put the bag on the table and started to take out the food. Hoping Jake had changed his mind, she turned around and saw him sitting in the driver's seat. Frantically, she reached inside her pocket. No keys.

Anna sprinted to the Jeep where Jake sat in the driver's seat, hunched over the steering wheel and gripping the keys in the ignition.

"Going somewhere?" she asked, panting.

He sighed and threw his body back against the seat.

She leaned across his chest and yanked the keys from the ignition, then went back to the picnic bench. So much for eating outside.

She put the food back into the bag and returned to the Jeep. "I'll eat in here."

He sighed but didn't move.

"Ah, I'm waiting."

He climbed over the console and plopped down in the passenger seat.

Anna got in and shut the door. With the bag on her lap, she pulled out a turkey sandwich, removed the cling wrap, and took a bite.

She and Jake picked up where they left off—in silence.

Anna's sweet tooth flared up the moment her teeth sank into Mrs. Elardo's homemade cookies. She held back, eating only two, then scolded herself when consuming a third cookie.

Since her departure from Channel 3 News, morning runs on Delaware Avenue were no longer part of her fitness routine. Five pesky pounds had appeared more quickly than she'd expected. But her incidental weight gain didn't preclude her from opening the lid to the container tucked in the console. The baked goods were so delicious, she devoured a fourth cookie while driving west on the I-90.

While Anna couldn't stop eating, Jake hadn't started. Nothing inside Mrs. Elardo's care package drew his interest. Not the turkey sandwiches or the bag of potato chips. Eventually, he'd cave. He'd have to. He was a teenage boy. They were always hungry.

Anna held the open container in front of him. "Want one?" The blended smells of sugar and chocolate filled the car. Any minute he'd fold like a deck of cards.

"I'm not hungry," he mumbled, staring out the window.

Not hungry? He's got to be famished by now!

"Are you sure? They're really good." She inched the container closer to his face.

"I said I'm not hungry!"

Anna put the Tupperware back in the console and

snapped the lid shut. "Fine. But we've got another four hours to go, and I'm only stopping one more time for gas."

"So?" he replied.

"So...four hours is a long time. Even longer when you haven't eaten all day."

Jake slouched down, arms crossed tightly against his chest.

Anna had spent the first half of the trip in silence; she refused to spend the second half the same way. She turned on the radio, hoping a good song would lighten the mood.

The preset stations for the Buffalo region produced nothing but static. She slowly hit the arrow key on the radio panel, stopping at each station that came in clearly. A commercial for a shoe sale—no thanks. Another commercial, this time for a small construction company. She kept rapidly pressing the arrow key, finally stopping at an oldies station playing Elvis Presley's "Suspicious Minds." Anna bobbed her head to the beat of the song.

Jake curled his lips. "Isn't there anything else on?" His tone was agitated.

She tapped her thumbs against the steering wheel in time with the song. "Probably, but I like this."

"Old people listen to this crap."

She raised her eyebrow. "I'm not old, and it's not crap. It's a classic."

"Is this part of my punishment? Torture by a fat, dead guy?"

"Ah-ha! You do know a little about the King of Rock and Roll."

Jake slouched farther down in his seat. "Whatever."

"Yeah, yeah. Whatever," she said, mocking him.

Jake had said more in two minutes than the entire time they'd been on the road. Not the best conversation, but it was a start.

"The shoe commercial was better than this," he muttered under his breath.

In response to his sarcasm, Anna turned up the volume and continued bobbing her head and tapping the steering wheel to the beat of the music.

Forty dollars filled the gas tank to the brim. The rest stop outside of Montpelier, Ohio, was the last planned stop. Two hours to go, and Anna would be in Garrison.

She paid the cashier and hopped back into the Jeep. This time, she'd remembered to take the keys out of the ignition.

Jake hadn't said a word since the Elvis incident. She wasn't surprised.

As she crossed the Indiana state line, her hands grew clammy. Moisture from her palms left a streak on the steering wheel.

Fort Wayne was the last metro city to drive through. From there on, it was nothing but rural communities for fifty miles. Lush grass surrounded dairy farms appearing small in the distance. Acres of crops, one after another, reached their peak for the season. Midwest memories came flooding back to her. Most of them were good, and a few were so bad that she'll never forget them.

Driving south on Route 69 with the cruise control set at seventy miles per hour, Anna reminded herself the reason for her return: to finish the book.

Chapter Fifteen

The green and white sign on the side of the road read *Muncie Exit 41*.

Anna veered the Jeep into the right lane and took the exit. Once she passed through the small college town, the highway whittled down from four to two lanes. The distance between neighboring homes increased the farther she drove, and the familiar stench of cow manure greeted her. And Jake.

"Holy crap. That's disgusting."

She glanced at him, watching him scrunch his face in utter repulsion.

"It's not that bad. You'll get used to it."

He covered his nose with his hand. "Yeah, right."

Letting up on the gas pedal, Anna passed the large billboard she had posed in front of when she was a little girl.

WELCOME TO GARRISON, INDIANA
A Friendly Town

Eight years had done a number on the royal blue sign, now faded from the sun.

A queasy wave rippled through her stomach, the same kind she used to get on a first date.

She was back home.

Anna drove five miles slower than the speed limit on Main Street, taking in the town's business district. The one mile stretch led her to the end of the street where the light gray siding on the corner of Claire Hartman's diner stuck out from behind a group of willow trees.

The Jeep's tires kicked up small clouds of dust from the gravel in the unpaved parking lot. She removed her sunglasses to get a better look at the old-fashioned eatery shaped in a simple rectangle.

The large white sign with black letters read, *Claire's*. Six symmetrically planted boxwood bushes—three on each side—flanked the entrance beneath the front windows. A discolored OPEN sign hung on the glass door.

Halfway out of the Jeep, an amalgam of smells awakened Anna's senses. The familiar aroma seeped from the diner, forcing her to take notice of what was once an integral part of her life. She again had to remind herself she was really back in Garrison when she heard a voice coming from the diner entrance.

"Well, it's about time."

She quickly turned around to see Claire Hartman

standing in the doorway wearing a sleeveless pink-checkered blouse, jean shorts, and sneakers. Immediately, Anna ran into her embrace. Claire hugged her tight, tighter than anyone had hugged her in a long time.

"Let me look at you," she said, stepping back. Holding back tears with a half grin on her face, she shook her head. "Eight years. Eight long years."

Anna studied her friend's features starting with her dirty-blond hair pulled back in a ponytail. The splattering of freckles around her nose nearly blended into her tanned complexion, and there were a few new wrinkles around the corner of her eyes and mouth.

"Claire, you look great."

"Na, just older I suppose." She pushed a few wavy strands of hair from her forehead. "How was the drive?"

Anna sighed. "It wasn't without a few challenges."

The door slammed shut. Jake leaned up against the Jeep.

She held her breath as they walked toward the angry teen.

"Hey there, I'm Claire. You must be Jake."

His eyes dropped to the ground as he kicked the small stones back and forth.

Anna let out a nervous giggle. "It was a long ride."

"Yeah, I imagine it was. Well, welcome to Garrison. I think you'll enjoy your stay here."

He rolled his eyes.

Uh-oh. Big mistake.

Claire's hands landed on her hips. Her squinted eyes locked onto his while taking slow strides closer to the teen. "Did you just roll your eyes at me?" she asked, drawing out her accent and leaning into him.

Anna slid in front of Jake as if she were a human shield. "So, where's Denny?"

"Ah...he's around here somewhere," she said, but she kept her eyes on Jake. Cupping her hands around her mouth she shouted, "Hey Denny! Get on out here. Anna's home!"

Footsteps sounded behind Anna and before she could turn, a pair of hands grabbed her waist, lifted her off the ground, and twirled her around. "There's my Anna Banana!"

Anna screeched. "Denny, you haven't changed a bit."

He put her down and hugged her, grunting as he squeezed her. "Neither have you. You're just as pretty as the last time I saw you... eight years ago."

"Okay, okay, I get it. It's been a long time."

Claire affectionately tapped her husband's shoulder. "Come on, Denny. Leave our girl alone."

A hearty laugh came from the depths of his belly. "Ah, she knows I'm just teasing."

Anna motioned to her reticent travel companion. "Denny, this Jake. Jake, Denny."

The brawny man extended his hand. "Nice to meet you."

"Hi," the teen replied just above a whisper.

"Well, I know one thing, I'm starving. Claire, we're going

to the cottage to unpack and freshen up. We'll be back in about an hour."

"The place is all fixed up," she said.

Anna leaned in for another hug. "Thanks, you're the best."

"Don't mention it, sweetie."

She and Jake got into the Jeep. She leaned out the window and said, "See you at supper."

"No rush. Take your time."

Anna drove out of the diner parking lot and headed for the cottage.

As Anna unloaded the suitcases from the trunk, Jake sat slumped in the front seat.

"Could you give me a hand?" she called from the back of the Jeep.

He huffed for what seemed like the millionth time. Slowly, he got out of the Jeep, slung his backpack over his shoulder, and shuffled his feet across the gravel driveway.

Anna handed him his suitcase and managed to tuck a piece of luggage from her set under each of her arms. He followed at a distance as they walked toward the porch.

Staring at the old cottage with its peeling paint and unkept landscaping, Anna sensed the loss of the lives that had once been inside. Travelers passing through Garrison on their way to bigger cities had once found solace in the quaint country cottage until more and more franchise hotels popped up offering low rates and better amenities. But no matter the competition, Claire hadn't been able to bring herself to shut down the cottage. Too many memories. The rental property had been about hospitality, not profit.

Squeaks escaped from each wooden plank they stepped on leading to the porch. Anna had to put down some of the luggage and juggle the rest as she used her foot to prop open the screen door and unlock the inner one. Once inside, she dropped the heavy suitcases on the floor. "Here we are. Home sweet home. At least for the next few months."

She went back outside to get the rest of her bags. When she returned, Jake hadn't moved. He stood in the family room, scanning the area while his mouth hung open.

He grunted in disgust. "You're kidding."

"What did you expect?" she said, setting down the bags. "A five-star hotel and private balcony?"

"I thought she said she fixed the place up."

"Her name is Claire, not she."

He investigated his new surroundings. "Is this the TV?"

"Yeah."

He approached the small unit. "Where's the remote?"

"There isn't one."

As if he'd come face to face with an alien, Jake cautiously touched the two thin metal rods sticking up from behind

108

the television. "What are these things?"

"Antennas. Some people call them rabbit ears. They help with the reception. There's no cable or satellite."

He pointed to the clunky, avocado green phone on the end table. "Why aren't there buttons?"

"It's a rotary phone." Anna picked up the receiver and waived it in the air. "Still works."

His interrogation shifted to the furniture. "This couch. It's...so ugly! What is it? A hundred years old or something?"

"Who cares what it looks like as long as you can sit on it?"

Appalled at his living conditions for the summer, Jake threw his arms in the air. "This place is a dump!"

If his words were meant to hurt her, they didn't.

"It's cozier than Wyatt. Or a jail cell."

Anna wasn't blind. Jake was only fifteen. Antiquated features like rabbit ears and rotary phones were common generations before he was born. His reaction was natural. It meant he was a normal teenager.

From the shag carpet to the flowered wallpaper, he criticized, complained, and pointed out every faulty detail he could think of.

Funny how the script flips. He'd spent the ride ignoring her. Now, he wouldn't shut up. Maybe the silent treatment wasn't so bad after all.

Anna picked up one of her suitcases. "Look, I know this

isn't what you're used to. I get it, this stuff is old and outdated. But people around here live simple lives. That's the way it's always been. That's the way it will always be."

"Is that why you left?" he asked with a smug look. "Couldn't take living in squalor huh, Anna?"

She froze. Suddenly, the suitcase felt like it was filled with cement.

It never crossed her mind that Jake would pry. Her private life was her business. She wasn't about to divulge information to an irate kid.

"You can have that room," she said, pointing down the hallway. "Second door on the left." She motioned to his suitcase. "Go unpack."

He went to his room and slammed the door shut.

The last folded shirt was stacked neatly in the dresser drawer with the rest of Anna's summer clothes. All four suitcases were emptied in twenty minutes giving her time to freshen up before dinner.

After brushing her teeth and fixing her hair, she put on a pair of khaki shorts and a purple T-shirt. Sitting on the edge of the bed as she slipped on her sandals, the turquoise curtains caught her eye and triggered a memory.

Claire had hung them up and done most of the work that day. Anna helped in ways a ten-year-old girl could—

handing her the rod and screws to put the hooks in the wall. It wasn't much, but she'd felt useful.

Holding the fabric in her hand, she pulled the hem of the curtain toward her nose, curious if twenty years had extinguished the sweet fragrance of the cotton polyester blend. She closed her eyes and sniffed the material, pleased to discover the familiar smell.

Peering out the window, clinging to the fabric, the grassy parcel of land behind the cottage captivated her attention. Parting the curtains, she stuffed a clump of material inside the wall hook on each side of the window. She stared at the acre of property as a flock of birds flew in unison across the late afternoon sky. A light breeze gently swayed the tips of the leafy maple trees.

She could have stayed at the window until sunset, but hunger pulled her away from the simplistic life unfolding before her. She glanced at her watch; it was ten after six. Claire was expecting them for supper.

Anna stacked the red luggage set on the closet floor, left the room, and went to Jake's room. She knocked on the bedroom door and opened it before receiving an invitation to enter. She gasped at the sporadic patches of tan carpet poking through a sea of clothing.

Teenagers are known for being slobs—especially boys. Anna didn't doubt that was the case for Jake, but he'd only been in the room a few minutes. His messy antic was deliberate.

She tiptoed around shirts, pants, and underclothes strewn across the floor. Jake was lying on the bed with his arms folded behind his head.

She pointed to the clothes. "You call this unpacked?"

Staring at the ceiling, he coolly replied, "You said unpack. You didn't say put it away."

"You know what I meant."

"Why are you making such a big deal out of this?"

"Because I don't like them on the floor, that's why."

"Well I do," he said, wiggling himself into a more comfortable position. "Get used to it."

Jake could huff, sigh, pout and say, "whatever," all he wanted, but he wasn't going to talk to her like that.

She pointed her finger at him. "Put your clothes away." Her tone was firm.

He darted upright from the bed. "It's my stuff, and I'll put it where I want!" He grabbed the open suitcase and hurled it at her like a madman. She turned her body and shielded her head with her hands. Luckily, his aim was off. The flying luggage missed her by mere inches.

Anna opened her eyes, slowly lowering her forearms from her face. Like a grisly car accident, she had to look and see his face. All the anger, all the rage buried deep with nowhere to go, finally had risen to the surface.

He strode toward her, got right in her face, and screamed. "You're not my mother. You're nothing to me. You don't want me here. I'm just a charity case to you. The pathetic kid no one wants!"

Nothing had prepared Anna for the vehement confrontation. Not a lesson in the foster care manual. Not a pep talk from Henry. Not even inside information from Stephanie. She hadn't signed up for this. She was in way over her head. Maybe Stephanie was right. Maybe there was more to Jake than what she wanted to believe.

Anna headed for the door. Her hand was on the knob when she stopped and turned around. Jake's glazed eyes were on the verge of crying and his mouth clenched in fury. He stood panting, winded from his outburst.

She took a deep breath, forcing herself to stay calm. "This was supposed to be a solo mission for me. And, yeah, I do feel sorry for you. It's not fair what happened to your parents. The world can be a very lonely place without people who love you. No one understands that like you."

She expected him to lash out again, but when he didn't, she continued.

"For some unexplainable reason, this is how it's going be. So, I suggest we do our best to get along and make the next two and a half months bearable. And since I'm responsible for you, you're going to follow the rules."

Jake's countenance fell. "You're not sending me home?"

His tone made it sound like he wanted to go to Wyatt. But Anna wasn't ready to wave the white flag.

"Nope. You're stuck with me."

He sat on the bed.

"Now, put these clothes away in that big, brown gizmo over there called a dresser. Then we're going to the diner. If you're not ready by the time I leave, I'm going without you. If you don't want to eat, that's your choice. You can go hungry."

She pushed the door wide open. "You have ten minutes."

Chapter Sixteen

Tiny chrome bells attached to the metal bar of the door rattled against the glass as Anna walked in the diner.

Claire called out from behind the partition separating the kitchen from the dining area. "You're just in time, food's done."

"Great. My stomach's been gurgling since Fort Wayne." Anna couldn't wait to eat a home-cooked meal.

Jake lagged behind her. Either he'd ended his hunger strike, or her talk had some impact. He'd finished putting away all his clothes with a few minutes to spare. Whether or not he'd folded them was another story for another day. She wasn't going to rummage through his drawers. She preferred to fight one battle at a time.

Like the exterior, the diner looked the same on the inside as it had when Anna left Garrison. The same cherry red booths took residence along the building's periphery. The same stainless steel stools at the counter. And of course, the photographs. Lots of photographs. Vintage photos, modern photos, celebrity photos, autographed photos, and photos of residents and landmarks. All shapes and sizes creating a unique wallpaper of life inside and outside of Garrison.

Some people collect coins, others stamps or baseball

cards. Claire collected photographs. She didn't just love hanging pictures, she loved taking them too. If not for the diner, Anna had no doubt her lifelong friend would've made a name for herself in the photography world.

Admiring the collage brought a smile to her face. But when her eyes landed on a particular black and white photo, the surrounding pictures disappeared from her vision. Only one mattered—the one of her mother and Claire with their arms around each other as they held a one-dollar bill.

Anna's bottom lip quivered. She tried pulling herself away from the wall, but her legs were paralyzed.

A whoosh sounded from the swinging kitchen doors as the Hartmans came into the dining area, each carrying two plates of food.

"Supper's ready," Claire said, setting down the plates at a corner booth. She saw Anna and went to her. "Darlin'?" Gently, she touched her arm. "Supper's ready."

Anna flashed a half-hearted smile and followed Claire to the booth.

She slid over to make room for Jake, who plopped down next to her. Claire came back from the kitchen with four glasses of water on a small tray, then sat next to Denny.

The succulent smell of comfort food drew Anna's attention away from the photograph for the time being. Dipping her head down, she closed her eyes and took a whiff of the large portions covering the plate. "Mmmm.

Meatloaf, garlic mashed potatoes, roasted carrots, and buttermilk biscuits. My favorite."

Claire smiled. "Like I'd forget."

Jake picked up his fork and examined his dinner. He broke off a piece of meatloaf and went to take a bite when Denny politely stopped him.

"Son?"

He looked up.

"We give thanks before eating."

The teen's cheeks turned pink. He set his fork down and looked at Anna. "Do I have to?"

She gave a subtle nod, even though he wasn't the only one reluctant to pray. So far, it was all they agreed on.

The Hartmans joined hands and closed their eyes. Out of respect for her friends, Anna partially bowed her head while Jake watched the religious tradition unfold.

Denny led the prayer. "Lord, we thank you for this food. We pray that it blesses our bodies. We thank you for your provision. And Lord, we especially want to thank you for the opportunity to share this meal tonight with family. In Jesus' name. Amen."

Claire gave a hearty, "Amen." She added, "We certainly have a lot to be thankful for."

"That we do," Denny said, breaking apart his biscuit with his fingers. He looked at Jake, who wasn't eating. "Well, go on. Dig in before it gets cold." He bit into the biscuit and smiled.

Anna went straight for the meatloaf. She occasionally moaned with delight, savoring each bite as if the meal was slated to be her last.

After dinner, Claire began to remove the dirty dishes from the table.

Anna wiped her mouth with a napkin. "That was the best meal I've had in years."

"It was okay," Jake muttered.

"You wouldn't think so by lookin' at your plate," Claire said, adding his dish to the pile. She shot him a smirk and carried the stack to the kitchen.

Jake had eaten every morsel, right down to the crumbs from the flakey biscuits. Now that he'd tasted Claire's cooking, there was no turning back. Her food was like a powerful drug—one meal and he'd be back for more.

Anna glanced at her watch. It was seven o'clock. "I hate to eat and run, but we better get going."

"Oh, no you don't!" Claire yelled from behind the counter. Returning to the booth, she had four dessert plates in her hand. "Not before dessert. Peach pie, baked it fresh this morning."

Anna's mouth watered. There was no way she could resist the homemade dessert topped with vanilla ice cream.

"Well, okay. Only because you went to all that trouble," she said with a wink.

Claire chuckled. "And a cup of green tea to go with it?"

"I'd love one."

Claire lightly tapped Jake's back. "How about a cold glass of milk to wash down that pie?"

He twirled his fork. "Milk is for kids."

"Oh, I see. Maybe a shot of whiskey is more to your likin'." Claire hadn't lost her sass.

Jake looked up and sighed. "I'll take the milk."

She smiled. "That's what I thought. Be right back."

After dessert, the Hartmans brought Anna up to speed on the comings and goings in Garrison since she'd left. The conversation bored Jake who chose to stare out the window at the empty parking lot.

Anna had nearly finished her second cup of tea when the sun began to set.

"Claire, everything was delicious, but we really have to get going."

Denny took a sip of his coffee. "Yeah, busy day tomorrow," he said, nodding his head at Jake.

The teen's forehead furrowed. "What do you mean?"

Denny stared at Anna with apologetic eyes for letting the cat out of the bag. He quickly gulped the rest of his coffee.

Claire, on the other hand, was blunt.

"Ya didn't tell him?"

"Tell me what?" Jake asked, even more puzzled.

"Since I'll be busy working on my book, Claire is going to let you work here. At the diner."

"What?" He slapped his palm against the table. "You're not serious!"

"It's better than sitting around all day doing nothing." Anna took another sip of tea. "You might as well do something productive."

"Oh yeah, right! What am I supposed to do around here that's so productive, huh?"

"Little bit of everything," Claire said. "Clean dishes, bus tables, take an order or two."

"How much are you paying me?"

"Nothing."

"What do you mean, nothing?"

"Just what I said, nothing."

"You can't do that!"

"I can too, cuz it's my diner," Claire shouted.

Anna put her hand on Jake's wrist to get his attention, but he yanked it away. She sighed. "Look, one of the stipulations of you coming with me is that you do community service. It's part of your sentence. Community service means you volunteer. You don't get paid."

The teen threw his body back against the cushioned booth like an angry toddler, his arms crossed tightly across his chest. "Sounds like slave labor."

"No, just an honest day's work." Anna picked up her mug and downed the last swig of tea. "I suggest you get a good night's sleep. You're going to need it."

Chapter Seventeen

Hunched over a large sink, Jake huffed as he rinsed a dirty dish and handful of silverware with hot water before putting them inside the dishwasher.

He pulled and tugged at the thick white apron tied around his waist, for no reason other than he wished he didn't have to wear it. It made him feel like a girl. A sissy. He wanted nothing more than to rip it off and throw it in the trash, but Claire insisted he keep it on.

Claire.

Three hours into his shift and one thing was certain. He couldn't stand her. Watching her cook behind the griddle, he hoped she'd burn herself on the hot surface. But he doubted that would happen.

Using a big metal spatula, she scooped out a slab of butter from a large bucket. She plopped it onto the hot surface where it turned into a pool of liquid in seconds. She reached up and grabbed two sheets of paper hanging from the ridged panel. She glanced at the scribbled diner shorthand before dumping a bowl full of eggs onto the buttered griddle. The metal spatula dinged and scraped against the hard surface as she cooked the mixture into a mound of fluffy scrambled eggs.

"I need another load-it-up and a large stack of hotcakes," a waitress said. She tore the order sheet from her tablet and clipped the paper into the ridge.

"You got it, hon," Claire replied. She pushed the giant mass of eggs off to the side then poured three large circles of hotcake batter onto the stove.

She moved effortlessly back and forth from the stove to the prep counter where large bins of cooked bacon, sausage, and French toast were waiting to be put on plates. Within minutes, the orders were done and on the ledge for the waitress to pick up when Claire noticed dirty dishes in the dining area.

She looked over her shoulder at Jake. "Five and six need clearing."

The dishwasher's piercing buzzer signaled the end of the cycle. Jake slid the door open. A cloud of steam escaped, coating his face and arms. He wiped away a layer of sweat above his brow with the back of his hand.

Hoisting the heavy crate filled with plates, mugs, glasses, and utensils from the dishwasher, he stumbled and lost his balance. The prep counter broke his impending fall.

Claire ripped off another order from the panel. "Come on, Jake, those tables need clearing now."

He set the crate down and grabbed the white bin used to transport dishes and silverware from the dining area to the kitchen. Walking past Claire, he mumbled in a low voice, "Get off my back."

She stopped pouring the hotcake batter in midair. "Excuse me, mister, what did you just say?"

"Nothing," he said, his head hanging down.

"Go on. Tables five and six."

A blast of air conditioning met him as he walked through the swinging door. The cool breeze felt so good that for a moment he forgot about the kitchen and Claire's hot temper. But the activity in the dining area brought him back to reality. Muffled conversations and the clanging sound of forks against plates and cups against tables was a bunch of noise he'd rather not hear. He sighed at the thought of spending all summer behind a sink full of dirty dishes in a sweltering kitchen.

Jake passed a booth with three teenage girls and heard, "There he is."

He felt their eyes watching him work. Casually, he turned his head in their direction. *Not bad looking... for a bunch of country girls.* They huddled close and whispered when his eyes met theirs.

He took his time wiping the table and snuck another peek when the blonde in the corner flashed him a sweet smile. His cheeks felt warm. His heart pounded.

Jake went to table six and turned around when he thought he heard one of them say, "He's cute."

After cleaning the table, he walked past their booth and was about to go through the swinging door when Claire set two plates on the partition.

"Jake, take these to table eight."

He placed the bin on the floor behind the counter, wiped his hands across his apron, and reached for the plates. Claire slid them back toward her. "Ah, wash your hands first, please."

He sighed and went into the kitchen where he did what he was told and then returned to the dining area. He stuck his hands in the air and twisted back and forth.

"That's more like it." She grinned and handed him the plates. "Table eight."

"Yeah, I got it."

He picked up the orders and walked past the girls' booth.

Setting the plates down in front of two elderly ladies at table eight, who couldn't have weighed more than ninety-five pounds each, they stared at the load-it-up combo and large stack of hotcakes. He swapped the plates, but their confused countenances remained.

"Hey, Jake!" Claire called out. "Over there," she said, pointing to the table to his right.

Two burly men with beards waved to get his attention.

"Oh, right." He removed the plates and took them to the right table.

Walking back to the counter he grumbled, "Is it always this busy?"

Claire snorted. "Wait 'til lunch."

"Why?" he asked, afraid to hear the answer.

"You'll see." She cocked her head toward the kitchen.

"You better head on back. Dishes are piling up."

The thought of another plate made Jake sick. He couldn't look at it, he didn't want to touch it, scrape food off it, put it away, nothing. He hated doing dishes. He hated cleaning up after people. He'd never get used to life in Garrison. He'd never get used to the diner, nor did he want to. Everything inside of him wanted to yell, "I quit!" and storm out the door, never to come back.

The only bright spot of an otherwise rotten day was the pretty girl in the booth. Picturing her smile made him smile. But she and her friends were gone, and he didn't know if he'd see her again.

On the way to the kitchen, the photo collage on the wall made him stop and take notice.

"They were so proud of that dollar."

Jake turned around when he heard Denny's voice. He pointed at the dark-haired woman in the photograph. "Who is she?"

"That's Lydia, Anna's momma. She was Claire's best friend. People say you shouldn't go into business with friends. But Lydia...she was different. You could trust her. And we did."

"Does she live around here?"

Glancing at the floor, Denny's tone turned solemn. "Not anymore, son."

"Did she move or something?"

Denny took a deep breath. "Lydia died eight years ago."

Chapter Eighteen

Anna's imagination ran wild. She envisioned broken plates and water gushing onto the kitchen floor. By the time she pictured a two-alarm fire, complete with raging flames and plumes of smoke billowing into the sky, she chuckled at the feigned drama she'd created.

If only that creativity would land on the pages of her book instead of being trapped in her head.

She took her laptop outside and sat on the rickety porch swing.

Jake was fine. She was sure of it. Claire would have called by now if his first day on the job was the disaster she'd conjured up.

Her bare feet dangled off the worn furniture as she pushed her toes against the floor. The swing swayed back and forth. The tattered awning sheltered her from the intense afternoon rays. A heat wave hovered over the Midwest. Meteorologists predicted a high temperature of eighty-eight.

Garrison was devoid of a body of water, large or small. Buffalo, on the other hand, was located along Lake Erie. On a hot day, a walk along the waterfront watching seasonal activities in action was a peaceful way to endure the heat.

Boats of all sizes and styles filled the Erie Basin Marina. Dozens of amateur and experienced sailors were on the lake in their boats by mid-morning for a leisurely nautical day. Seeing fishermen prepped with their tackle boxes, nets, and bait ready to cast their rods into the water hoping to reel in some big fish always reminded her of Denny.

He'd taken her on her first overnight fishing excursion three hours southwest of Garrison to Patoka Lake—the second largest reservoir in Indiana spanning Dubois, Crawford, and Orange counties.

To experience the full effect of the trip, he'd suggested they pitch a tent and sleep outside. But for an eleven-year-old girl, lying on the cold, hard ground with bugs roaming around wasn't the thrill of a lifetime. Denny let out one of his hearty chuckles when she told him how she felt. Then he got the next best thing—a cabin on the campsite.

The mass of water stocked with bass, bluegill, catfish, crappie, and walleye was the perfect spot to catch her first smallmouth bass. The seven-pound fish put up a fight, but she could count on Denny to help reel it in.

Her excitement immediately faded once the fish was in the net. She watched the sad, pathetic creature flop around, struggling to survive out of its aquatic environment. She didn't have the heart to kill it.

Anna looked at Denny but said nothing, hoping he'd read her mind. Thankfully, he had. He unfastened the hook, and she tossed the fish back in the water. And the next three.

Her future didn't include being a die-hard fisherman, that's for sure. But she looked forward to spending time with Denny at Patoka Lake every summer for their annual fishing weekend.

The motion from the porch swing slowed down. She couldn't have asked for a better place to write. The serene setting was like something out of a fictional story. No unwanted phone calls. No nosey neighbors. No city noises. Only the picturesque view of birds soaring across the bright blue sky.

Anna opened her laptop, retrieved the document, and began to type. Words turned into sentences, sentences led to paragraphs, and paragraphs produced pages. Finally, her story burst out of her like water shooting from a busted fire hydrant. She was in the zone, focused on the path ahead. Every writer knew what that zone felt like.

But when a red Toyota Camry slowed down and pulled in the driveway, the zone turned into a dead end.

Anna stood to her feet. Using her hand as a visor to block the sun, she squinted, trying to see who the driver was. She was too far away to get a clear view until he got out and shut the door.

"Hey there! I heard you were back."

Her stomach sank.

There were a few people in town Anna wanted to avoid. Pastor Gill Shaw was one of them. But there he was. Uninvited.

"It's been a while, Anna. How ya doing?"

Indeed, it had been a while. The shots of gray around the edges of his short, black hair proved it.

She politely smiled. "Can't complain. How're your wife and the girls?"

Shoving his hands in the pockets of his khaki shorts, he took a few steps forward. "Aww, good. Real good. Can't ask for a better partner in life than Erica. And the girls are doing great. Liv is fifteen. Emma's thirteen. They talk about boys, clothes, and take forever getting ready in the morning. Typical girl stuff, I suppose." He chuckled. "Ah, but they sure do keep life interesting."

"Teens will do that for you."

"That's for sure." He grinned. "You're getting a taste of that yourself. Heard you're taking care of a kid from back home. Jake is his name, right?"

So much for privacy.

"Yeah, that's right."

"How's that going?"

"Fine. We're doing fine."

If that clue wasn't clear enough for Pastor Gill to end the conversation, Anna was prepared to be more direct. Thankfully it was.

The following moments of awkward silence lasted only seconds but felt like hours. Glancing at the ground, he came clean.

"Listen, Anna, I've never been one for lying. I'm not

gonna say I happened to be in the neighborhood. That just wouldn't be true." He adjusted his glasses and continued. "We'd love to see you Sunday morning."

Anna never wanted to step foot inside another church unless it was for a wedding or funeral, and even those would be debatable.

"Thanks, but I can't. It was nice of you to think of me, but I have a lot to do. I'm...I'm really busy." Even she didn't believe the vague excuse.

His smile softened. "Is it too much to ask to give God a couple hours of your time?"

Anna tried coming up with a more viable reason. But when you're going up against a pastor, any excuse to skip church is moot. Besides, she didn't owe him anything. Not an explanation, not an excuse, and not the truth.

She looked at him as if he were a salesperson pitching a product she wouldn't buy no matter what. Her silence said his presentation had ended. It was time for him to leave.

"Well, invitation stands if you change your mind." A disappointed smile appeared on his face. "I best be heading back to the church."

He opened the car door then stopped.

Oh no, what now?

After a brief hesitation he merely said, "Welcome home."

Anna gave a flimsy wave goodbye as he drove away. Hopefully, he'd take the hint and not come back.

She picked up the laptop and went inside the cottage.

130

Chapter Nineteen

Nicotine had consumed Jake's thoughts since lunch. His ten minute afternoon break couldn't come fast enough. The time was minimal, but he'd take anything to get away from the sweltering kitchen and sneak in a much-needed cigarette.

Finally, two o'clock came.

The minute hand struck twelve and he made a beeline for the screen door in the back of the kitchen. Clanking pots and utensils drowned out the squeaky noise from the door when he opened it. The lifeless property behind the diner served as the perfect spot for privacy.

Jake glanced over his shoulder. He was alone. Riffling through his pocket for a pack of cigarettes and a lighter, he could almost taste the sweet tobacco. And soon he would for real.

One flick of his black lighter lit the cigarette. He took a drag and smiled with satisfaction as he exhaled. He didn't worry about the smoky stench on his clothes giving him away. The smell of food from the kitchen would cover it up and no one would be the wiser.

It had been two torturous days since his fingers held a cigarette to his lips. He was already thinking about his next one. He looked at the pack in his hands and counted eight sticks. No way that would stretch two months.

Bringing the lit cigarette to his mouth, he took another drag, pondering a plan to lift a pack from the drugstore down the road when footsteps shuffling against the gravel made him freeze.

"I been meaning to get that door fixed."

Jake rolled his eyes and turned around.

Claire stood with her hands curled up into fists on her hips. "Did I forget to mention there's no smoking here?"

"But I'm outside." He took another drag and exhaled.

Her slow strides toward him didn't intimidate him.

"Inside or out, I don't care." She ripped the smoldering cigarette out of his hand.

"Hey! Give that back!"

Claire stared him down.

"Look, I'm not hurting anyone."

"Just yourself." She dropped the stick and ground the butt into the dirt with the toe of her shoe. She held out her hand, palm up.

"That was my last one," he said.

She smirked. "Don't lie to me. It ain't worth it."

He huffed, reluctantly handing over the pack of Marlboros.

She motioned with her fingers for the rest of the paraphernalia. He huffed again—louder—slapping the lighter into her hand.

"Jake, if you wanna suck in smoke that bad, go stand in a burning building. Otherwise, this is my property, and I say there ain't no smoking. Inside or out."

She squeezed the pack in her hand and shook it. "One day, your lungs will thank me for this."

Claire went back to the dinner. Before going through the back entrance, she turned around and said, "Break's over." She let go of the metal screen door and it squeaked shut.

Jake rolled up his semi-wet apron and shoved it underneath the counter the minute Claire told him his shift was over. He bolted from the diner leaving behind the sound of chrome bells on the door banging into each other.

After eight hours of dirty dishes and clearing tables, the dumpy cottage seemed like paradise—something he thought he'd never admit to himself.

Sauntering down a desolate dirt road running parallel to Main Street, Jake savored the time alone. No more hick town chatter. No more scraping food-coated plates. No more buzzing dishwasher. And no more Claire barking out orders. Nails dragging across a chalkboard sounded better that twangy voice of hers.

"Jake, five and six need clearin'."

"Dishes are pilin' up."

"Break's over."

Bryce had ordered him around. Look where it got him. Stuck in the middle of nowhere, working all day at a cruddy diner, cleaning up after people.

Jake needed a smoke bad. He reached into his pocket when an image of Claire destroying the pack flashed before him. *"One day, your lungs will thank me for this."*

He blew a heavy sigh. Right now, his lungs were ticked at Claire Hartman. Stealing cigarettes was a risk. People in small towns all knew each other. A missing pack from the drugstore would make him the number one suspect.

Kicking loose stones gave him something to look at until he saw a woman standing at the entrance of Garrison Cemetery clutching the wrought iron archway.

He squatted behind a cluster of brush growing along the side of the road, waiting to see what she'd do next. The sun hit his eyes, blinding him momentarily. Blocking the rays with his hands, he slid out to get a better view, but she was gone.

Chapter Twenty

Jake stared at her from afar. He couldn't take his eyes off her no matter how hard he tried.

Her long, blond hair pulled back in a half ponytail complemented her fair skin and blue eyes that resembled the color of the sky. When she laughed, she tipped her head back and closed her eyes for a split second. She played with the straw in her soda glass, bouncing it up and down and using it to swirl the ice cubes around before taking a sip.

For the third time that week, the pretty girl and her friends had stopped in the diner around noon for lunch and a gab session. Standing behind the counter, Jake periodically bent down pretending to look for something.

You're being stupid! Just go over there!

The self-admonishment worked.

He grabbed a bucket and a rag and strode to the booth in front of them. The table was already clean, but they didn't know that.

Jake hated cleaning tables but gladly stuck his hands in the tepid water just to get the chance to be near the mystery girl from Garrison. He moved the rag in circles, hitting every square inch of the rectangular table, hoping to hear their conversation. He looked toward their booth out of the corner of his eye. They had stopped talking. He re-washed the surface again. Suddenly, they burst out into giggles.

His hopes were dashed at the thought they were laughing at him. But the pretty girl's gaze said otherwise when she flashed him a coy smile.

He desperately wanted to talk to her, to hear what her voice sounded like. Before he got the chance to find out, Claire placed three plates on the ledge.

"Jake, come back here for a sec."

What does she want now?

He tossed the threadbare rag in the bucket and went to the kitchen.

"Yeah?" he asked, walking through the swinging door.

"Wash your hands then take that order to table four."

His face scrunched. "Table four?"

"Yeah, table four," she said, pointing her finger. "Right over there."

Table four—the pretty girl's booth.

"Well, com' on, hustle! Food's getting cold."

Her mandate gave him a kick in the pants. She smiled as if she knew exactly what she was doing. "Don't keep the customers waiting."

After washing his hands, he took a large brown waiter's tray from the dining room for assistance. He hadn't mastered the art of carrying multiple orders at one time yet. Carefully, he arranged the plates on the oval piece of plastic, relieved to see three identical orders of cheeseburgers and fries.

At least I can't screw it up.

In one swift lift, he propped the oversized tray on his right shoulder, keeping it balanced as he picked up a metal fold-out stand against the wall.

Slowly, he walked toward the booth. His forearm pulsated from the weight of the tray. The rest of his body trembled in nervous fear.

He felt his back about to give out just as he flipped the stand into position and carefully set the tray on it. Reaching across the table, he handed the pretty girl her meal first. She met him halfway.

"Thank you," she said, taking the plate from him.

"You're welcome," he replied just loud enough to be heard. He gave her friends their plates and cleared his throat. "Do you need anything else? Ketchup? Napkins? Salt?"

The pretty girl pointed to the items already on the table.

What an idiot!

Heat rushed to the surface of his cheeks. "Oh, yeah. Right."

Without a word, he picked up the tray and folding stand, and went toward the kitchen feeling like a deflated balloon. His only shot and he'd blown it big time. He couldn't bear to turn around and see them make fun of his dopey comment.

"Mind if I get some change?"

He turned. The pretty girl stood at the register holding out a dollar bill. He took the money and opened the register. He swallowed past a large lump in his throat. This time, he put an imaginary muzzle over his mouth.

She waited patiently, tapping her short fingernails on the counter. "You're Jake O'Connor, right?"

He looked up. "Yeah, how'd you know?"

She smiled. "It's a small town."

He handed her four quarters.

"Thanks. I'm Melanie Thompson, by the way."

"Jake O'Connor."

She giggled. "I know."

Her accent was like Claire's only it sounded much cuter coming from her.

"You're from Buffalo, like Anna?"

"Small town, right?"

"Guess so," she said. "How long will ya be in Garrison?"

"Until the end of the summer."

"Oh, that's nice. Well, I'm sure I'll see ya again. My friends and I come to the diner a lot. So...I'll see ya around." She stuck her hand out. "Nice to meet you, Jake O'Connor."

He eagerly received her handshake. "You too, Melanie."

Her skin felt like velvet. The intoxicating smell of her floral-scented perfume made him drunk with happiness. The small dimple in her left cheek when she smiled was adorable. Jake wanted her to stand at the counter for the rest of his shift.

She turned around, and her friends mouthed the words, *ask him.*

She took a deep breath and faced Jake. "I was wondering, umm, would you like to go to youth group with me and my friends Thursday night? If you're not busy, that is."

He couldn't believe what he was hearing. Melanie Thompson asked him out!

A grin spread across his face. "Sure, why not?"

Chapter Twenty One

Steam rising from Anna's cup of green tea weakened as it dissipated in the air. She sipped the hot beverage without blowing on it as her eyes fixed on the bright orange sun hanging at the horizon. Insects fluttered all around. Tiny tree branches crackled beneath the feet of critters moving about in wooded areas. Nature sounded beautiful.

Gliding back and forth on the porch swing, she took another sip of tea as nocturnal birds conversed with each other. Listening to their incessant chatter, wondering what they were saying, a smile spread across her face. Their lives were simple.

The vast difference between city life and small towns like Garrison had hit Anna the first time she sat on the porch of her apartment building in Buffalo. The only nature she'd been exposed to that night were honking horns, sirens, and crowds of people. She never thought she'd get used to all the noise. If she had, she'd be back in her apartment instead of surrounded by Midwest serenity.

"Hey."

She turned around, surprised to see Jake. Every night after dinner, he went to his bedroom and didn't come out until morning.

Anna scooted over on the porch swing. There was enough room for two, but he walked past her and stood in the corner. She sipped her tea.

He looked at her like she was nuts. "How can you drink that stuff?"

She shrugged her shoulders. "It's refreshing."

"It's, like, eighty degrees out here."

"So?"

"How can it be refreshing?"

"Not cold refreshing, more like good memories refreshing."

He shot her a puzzled look. "What do you mean?"

There was no sarcasm in his voice. Not even a hint. Could his genuine inquiry lead to a real conversation without the attitude, the huffing, or saying "whatever"? There was only one way to find out.

She held up the cup. "This was my mother's favorite drink and it became mine too." Tracing the rim with her index finger, she continued. "Hot green tea with a thin slice of lemon."

Jake stood quietly, waiting to hear more.

"Momma and I had a lot of nice talks over a cup of green tea. It didn't matter how hot or cold it was outside. Sometimes we talked for hours about everything... And about nothing."

Her eyes watched the floating slice of lemon. Part of her wanted to keep talking about her mother, the other half told her to shut up. Her private life was none of Jake's business.

But the concrete wall he'd built around himself showed signs of deterioration. The small crack in the foundation was a way in. Not wanting to squash this progress, she switched topics. "So, what did you want to talk to me about?"

He let out a nervous snort. "What makes you think that?"

"Just a hunch."

Stuffing his hands in his jean pockets, he stared at the porch floor. His foot fiddled with a jagged piece of wood sticking up. His hesitation had her on the edge of her seat. Finally, he asked, "Do you know the Thompsons?"

"George and Helen?"

"I guess that's them," he said, still poking at the wood.

The question came as no surprise. Claire had informed Anna about the crush Jake had on Melanie. Tempted as she was to put him on the spot, she refrained.

"Yeah, I know them. I went to school with their oldest daughter, Cindy."

"Are they nice?" he asked.

Anna took a sip of tea then answered, "Yeah, they are. Their youngest daughter, Melanie, is about your age I think."

"Yeah, I met her at the diner. She's okay."

Anna held back a grin. Styles in music and clothes changed from generation to generation, but teenage boys would never stop hiding their true feelings from girls.

"She asked me if I wanted to go to youth group." He

waved his hand in front of his face as if he swatted at a fly. "But I'm not sure I want to."

"Youth group, huh? You don't strike me as the youth group type."

"Yeah, I know." He sighed. "Then again, there's nothing else to do around here. TV is full of static. There's not even a radio to listen to."

Jake's cryptic way of asking permission amused her.

"It's all right with me. Just be back by ten."

"I can go?"

"Sure." Then Anna said something that took both of them by surprise. "I trust you, Jake."

His face softened. Another crack. Two in one night.

Jake walked briskly across the porch. "I'm going to go call her. You know, just to tell her I'm tagging along." He opened the screen door. "Hey, Anna?"

"Yeah?"

He turned around. "What's youth group?"

She tilted her head up and closed one eye like she was thinking. "In a nutshell, teenagers hanging out at church."

His eyebrows rose. "It's a religious thing?"

"Pretty much, but not as stuffy as church on Sundays."

"It's still better than hanging out here." He quickly retracted his words. "I mean, not that it's horrible here or anything."

Anna smiled. "I was your age too. I know what you meant."

He gave a crooked smile and went inside.

She listened to the faint sound of him dialing Melanie's number followed by a muffled conversation. She finished what was left of her tea and grinned.

Ah, young love.

Chapter Twenty Two

Jake had cleared the dirty dishes from table seven when Claire emerged from the kitchen carrying two plates. The lunch rush had finally subsided.

An influx of customers had kept him extra busy forcing him to skip his morning break. He worked diligently, bouncing back and forth between the kitchen and the dining area since his shift started at eight o'clock.

"Here you go, hon," Claire said. She set the plates down at an empty booth next to him. "Take a break and have something to eat."

Jake stashed the bin behind the counter. "Great. I'm starved." He plopped down in the booth.

"Mind if I join ya?" she asked, sitting down.

More of a statement than a question, he shook his head indicating it was fine with him—not that he had a choice. He certainly couldn't tell her to get up and go somewhere else. That would be suicide.

Claire closed her eyes and bowed her head. Jake followed suit, except for the eyes. He kept them open.

Talking to something he couldn't see didn't make sense to him. But what could it hurt? He deemed the ritual as extra practice before youth group with Melanie and her friends. The more opportunities he participated in prayer, the more he'd fit in with the other teens. He hoped.

Claire began. "Heavenly Father, thank you for the food you provided for Jake and me. Thank you for blessing it and for the strength we receive from it. In Jesus' name. Amen."

He sank his teeth into the meaty chicken salad sandwich coated in a creamy mayo and Dijon mustard blend. He couldn't decide which meal was the best—the one in front of him, the grilled cheese with ham and fries, the BLT and potato salad, or the patty melt and onion rings. The meals were simple but were the best he'd tasted in a long time.

They ate in silence until Claire mentioned Melanie's visit to the diner earlier that morning. Jake smiled before taking another bite of his sandwich. Being in the same room with Melanie for five minutes put him in a good mood for the rest of the day. His sporadic whistling while loading and emptying the dishwasher was proof.

Claire kept up the small talk and gave Jake a crash course in Garrison history with tidbits like the fire at the Town Hall in 1966, the undefeated high school boys' basketball team that captured the regional title in 1982, and the town's annual week-long birthday bash celebration with festivals, reenactments, and outings.

"You know a lot about this town, don't you, Claire?" he asked.

"Been here my whole life."

Jake paused, then found the courage to ask about Lydia.

"So, what happened to Anna's mom?"

Claire looked up from her plate. She immediately stopped chewing and stared at him as if she'd come face to face with a ghost. Placing her sandwich back on her plate, she swallowed, picked up a napkin, and wiped the corners of her mouth.

"I mean, I know she died. Denny told me. But what happened? What's the big secret?"

"There's no secret."

"Okay, then what happened?"

"I take it you didn't ask Anna?"

"No. The only thing she said about her mom was they had a lot of good talks when they drank tea. And I saw her at the cemetery."

Claire's eyes grew wide. "Did I hear ya right? She was actually *in* the cemetery?"

"Not really. Kinda like standing at the entrance. She didn't see me."

"Oh." She bit into her sandwich.

Jake stared at Claire. "Are you going to tell me what happened?"

She set the sandwich on the plate. "Me and Lydia were best friends since the first grade. When we were growing up, women around here didn't go to college unless they wanted to be a teacher or a nurse. For the rest of us, you'd graduate, find a man, get married, and have kids. We started the diner practically out of high school. A few years later, an attractive man stopped in. We knew he wasn't from around here. Someone that charming had outsider written all over him. He had that city look to him. Know what I mean?"

Jake nodded like he understood.

"Come to find out, he was a lawyer from Chicago heading to Indianapolis for a convention. He took to Lydia real fast." Claire giggled. "Then again, who didn't? Lydia was beautiful, that's for sure. Long dark brown hair—almost black—big brown eyes, and skin like silk."

Jake took another bite of his sandwich as she continued.

"On his way back from the convention, he stayed in town for a while. He and Lydia were inseparable. I swear, they were the most attractive couple I'd ever laid my eyes on."

Squeezing the crumpled napkin in her hand, Claire snorted in disgust. "Then one day he just left. Didn't tell her he was gonna, just up and gone. Left her a stupid note, the spineless weasel. Said they were just two different people from different worlds. Poor thing was heartbroken."

"Then what?" Jake asked. "How did she...you know...die?"

Staring out the window, Claire wiped away the tears forming in her eyes and sniffled. "Look, Jake, it's not my place to say. I've said too much already."

"But everyone knows she died. What does it have to do with that guy?"

"You have to understand, Lydia's death is a touchy topic for all of us. Especially Anna. Sometimes things are best left unsaid. This is one of them."

Claire picked up her plate with her half-eaten sandwich and handful of chips. "You best be finishin' up. Break's almost over." She walked back into the kitchen.

Jake took a small bite of his sandwich, wondering if he'd ever know the truth.

Chapter Twenty-Three

"Here you go, Claire. A shot of cream and two teaspoons of sugar."

"The only way I like it." She took the piping-hot mug from Anna's hands. "Thanks, darlin'."

She blew over the coffee's surface and impatiently took a sip before it had a chance to cool off, then winced when the beverage hit her lips.

Anna sat next to her on the porch swing. Staring at the cup of green tea in her hands made her think of her mother's dislike for coffee. She'd tried getting past the bitter bean taste, dousing it with sugar and cream, creating a mixture as white as the cup. But she just couldn't acquire a taste for it. Anna shared in her assessment as she looked intently at the clusters of stars in the sky. "You don't see nights like this in Buffalo, that's for sure."

"If ya visit more often–"

"We're having a good time, Claire. Let's not ruin it with criticism about my eight-year hiatus."

She playfully tapped Anna's arm. "Come on now, I had to take a shot."

Anna knew her friend meant no harm. It was just her way of saying she missed her.

Claire sipped her coffee, then switched topics. "So, tonight's the big night. Jake's at youth group with Melanie."

"Yep," Anna replied with an unsure sigh.

"Think he's having a good time?"

Bringing the cup to her lips, she paused. "If he's with Melanie Thompson, he's having a good time." She took a sip, then continued. "They could be together in a landfill during a rainstorm and it would be the best night of his life."

The last time Jake had been to church was for his mother's funeral two years earlier.

Church to him was a formal, boring place. A poorly lit room where quiet parishioners gathered on Sundays to ease their guilty consciences after engaging in sinful activity during the week. In the grand scheme of things, the reasons they went didn't matter, only the anticipation for the service to end.

But when he walked inside the Garrison Community Church, an upbeat song greeted his ears. The tune's tempo lured him away from the group he was with and drew him toward the sanctuary. He hid behind the open doors, careful not to be seen as he watched young musicians bang out a quick rehearsal. He counted two guitarists, a drummer, keyboard player, and one vocalist. The whole thing was pretty weird. Church music was supposed to be an old lady playing the organ, not kids in a rock band.

"Hey, Jake!" Melanie waved her hand in the air from across the hallway. "Wanna shoot some pool?"

Pool? At church? Now he was even more curious. "Sure."

He followed Melanie, Emma, and Liv across the small atrium to the fellowship hall filled with pool tables, dartboards, an air hockey table, and video game stations with Xbox and PlayStation.

Melanie gathered the balls from the pockets at a vacant table. She used the plastic triangle to rack while Jake grabbed two wooden cues hanging in pegs on the wall. He handed her one.

"How about you break?" she said.

"Okay."

Standing behind the arranged balls, Jake chalked the end of his stick, then leaned over the table and focused on the white ball. His powerful shot sent three solid colored balls sailing into a side and two corner pockets.

"I think I got my work cut out for me," Melanie joked.

"Na, just a lucky shot."

As they continued their game, an audience formed around them. The match came down to one ball apiece and the eight ball. Jake sank his last solid ball into the side pocket and ended the game with the eight ball rolling slowly into the corner pocket.

"Great shot," said a guy standing behind him.

Jake turned around. "Thanks."

152

Melanie made the introductions. "Nick, this is Jake O'Connor."

Nick stretched out his hand. "Nice to meet you." He pointed to his buddy. "This is Shane."

Jake shook their hands.

"Wanna play a game of darts? You and Melanie against me and this guy." He pointed to his friend with a smirk.

"Sounds good to me," Melanie said. "How about it, Jake? Let's show these two how it's done."

He smiled. "Lead the way." He went around the table and took the cue from her. "I can put that away for you."

She blushed at his gesture. "Why, thank you, Jake."

After their dart game, the teens went into the sanctuary.

Jake was having so much fun with Melanie, he didn't want to go to the service. He felt like they were on a real date, even though they were at church. He feared the feeling would end once they got into the religious stuff.

The three girls and three guys took up the entire section of seats in the second row. Jake made sure he got a seat next to Melanie.

The drummer clanked his sticks together in the air three times before lyrics appeared on a supersized monitor on the wall at the altar.

When the band started playing, Melanie leaned over and whispered to Jake, "This is the worship part. I think you'll like the songs. Our band's pretty good."

The teens stood up. Jake watched everyone around him

sing and clap, two things he found shocking yet intriguing. Tempted to join in, he felt like a phony, appearing as if he had done that sort of thing all the time. Eventually, people would call him out, he was sure of it. And why shouldn't they? He didn't go to church, especially one like Garrison Community.

The second time through the chorus, Melanie smiled at him and glanced down at the floor. He hadn't realized he'd been tapping his foot to the beat. She nodded her head. Her encouragement gave him confidence.

With a clumsy start, he mouthed the words, not actually singing, and incorporated a few off-beat claps. Sure, he wasn't the most musical kid there. A dog howling was more in tune than he was. But it didn't matter. He liked the Christian song's edgy rock beat. It was a far cry from the hard, violent lyrics he usually listened to.

Looking around the sanctuary, he felt welcomed. He felt safe. He hadn't thought it was possible to feel that way in church, but he did. And it made him feel good. As good as he'd felt in a very long time.

The band played three more songs, then Emma gave a quick overview of upcoming events.

The teens went back to the fellowship hall where a dozen chairs formed a large semi-circle in the middle of the room. Pastor Gill Shaw stood in the doorway entrance high-fiving and shaking hands with each person who walked past him. Jake was stunned by the minister's casual attire of jeans, a printed T-shirt, and sandals.

With his Bible still in hand, Pastor Gill moved into the middle of the circle and stood with his arms open as if ready to embrace someone with a hug. "I wanna thank you for coming out tonight. As always, it's great to see your smiling faces. Now that you're on summer break, I reckon there's more to smile about."

The group chuckled.

He continued. "I'd also like to welcome Jake O'Connor who's visiting us from Buffalo. Jake, it's great to have ya here."

Every pair of eyes looked in Jake's direction. The teens welcomed him with hearty applause.

"Thanks," he said with a smile.

"God has put on my heart to let everyone here know that He has a plan for your life. No matter what has happened, no matter what you may have gone through, good or bad, God's love is like no other. We've all had disappointments. We've all done things we shouldn't have." He raised his eyebrows. "Even me. Yes, even your pastor has screwed up from time to time."

He paused as if he were waiting for instructions on what to say next.

"It's not uncommon for us to think we can fix it on our own. That we can figure it out by ourselves. That we don't need anyone's help."

Jake listened intently to the passionate words full of life

coming out the pastor's mouth. He'd always thought religion was about heaven and hell. God's love was never a main focus. Until now.

Pastor Gill gripped his Bible. "Truth is, we can't do it on our own. And that's okay. Because it's only through God's strength and His power in us that we can get to where *He* wants us to go. God wants you lean on Him. Proverbs chapter 3, verses 5 and 6 says, 'Trust in the Lord with all your heart. Lean not on your own understanding, in all ways acknowledge Him.' What a relief to know that He has our backs. And those times you do mess up, He's got your back again. He forgives every single time. He makes things right, if you let Him. There's nothing He can't do."

Chapter Twenty-Four

Anna's eyelids fought hard to stay open. But the second they gave up, the screen door opened and kept her from falling into a deep sleep.

She quickly sat up, perched right on the couch with her laptop resting on her thighs as if she'd been working on her book. Jake came inside and shut the door.

"How was it?" she asked.

He shrugged his shoulders. "Good."

"Did you have fun?"

"Yeah."

Anna had hoped for a bit more than one-word answers. His vague responses meant either he really didn't enjoy it, or he was being a typical fifteen-year-old who didn't give details.

He walked past the couch and headed for the hallway. "I'm going bed. See you in the morning."

"Good night."

He went to his room and shut the door.

Anna didn't want to nag and ruin the small progress she'd made. She'd have to get creative and find another way to pull the information out of him later.

A dark-haired woman emerged from the crumpled car engulfed in glowing, orange flames. There wasn't a scratch on her.

Her hand met her mouth. She pressed the top of her fingertips to her lips and blew a gentle kiss. She turned and walked away, vanishing into the summer night.

Anna screamed. "Come back! Come back!" Then her body catapulted into an upright position. Struggling to catch her breath, panting like an overheated canine, she looked out the window. A bolt of lightning lit up the sky followed by a thunderous boom.

A dream. It was only a dream.

No, a nightmare—the same nightmare that haunted her for weeks after her mother's death. Only this nightmare was different. Her mother's illuminated spirit had stepped out of the vehicle—that had never happened before.

Anna's hands covered her face. She squeezed her eyes shut, trying to get another glimpse of her beautiful mother. But she couldn't. She was gone. Again.

Using the back of her hand, she wiped away the sweat on her forehead. Looking out the window, she watched the storm and listened to the synchronized beat of raindrops hit against the side of the cottage.

She sighed, collapsing backward onto the bed and stared at the ceiling.

Chapter Twenty Five

Anna sat at a stool at the counter and watched Jake in action.

"Here you go, Ed." He set the plate in front of the man reading the *Indianapolis Star*. "One load-it-up with extra-crispy home fries. Just the way you like them."

The customer folded the newspaper in half and tipped his baseball cap in gratitude. "Thanks, Jake."

The teen smiled. "You're welcome."

On his way back to the kitchen, he stopped at an empty booth and scooped up three sets of plates, utensils, and coffee mugs. He went behind the counter where he dumped them into a white bin. He hoisted it up and saw Anna at the end of the counter.

"What are you doing here?" He cocked his head to the side, squinting in suspicion. "Checking up on me, huh?"

"No. I needed a break and thought I'd hang out here for a bit."

Jake was quiet for a moment, then asked, "So... how's your book going?"

Her eyes widened. It was the first time he'd asked about her writing. The bin full of breakfast dishes hung down at his waist as he waited for an answer.

"It's coming along."

The corners of his lips curled up in a slight smile. He heaved the bin upward, then turned and walked through the swinging kitchen door.

Anna pondered the change in Jake who at one point had preferred juvenile hall over Garrison. She rubbed her hand across her eye, followed with a discreet yawn.

"Did the storm keep you up?" Claire asked from behind the partition.

The yawn must have been more obvious than Anna thought. "I guess so," she replied.

Not exactly a fib. The storm hadn't made it any easier to sleep. But it was the nightmare of her mother's car accident that had kept her awake. Every time she'd closed her eyes, she saw the burning car.

Claire came through the swinging doors and prepared a cup of hot green tea with lemon. "This oughta perk ya up," she said, sliding it across the counter.

Anna cupped her hands around the warm mug. "Thanks."

The tea did little to ease her mind.

Claire hovered over Anna like a mother hen. "You okay, darlin'?"

"I'm fine. Just tired."

Jake returned from the kitchen lugging a bucket of soapy water. He set it next to his feet and wrung the wet washrag that was inside. It was the perfect opportunity to change the subject.

a

"So, youth group went pretty good?"

He shrugged his shoulder. "Yeah, it was okay."

Anna's eyebrows rose at his matter-of-fact response "Just okay?"

"Yeah, what else do you want me to say?" He started cleaning the counter.

Jake spent three hours with a pretty girl. His night out had to be more than okay.

"Melanie had fun," Claire said, grabbing two lunch orders from the window. "She's already been by to see him."

"Claire!" Jake snapped.

"Oh, come on now. It's cute you have a girlfriend. And such a nice one at that." She sashayed past and delivered the two plates to the customers.

"Melanie's not my girlfriend."

"Maybe not yet," Claire said, tapping his shoulder, "but she will be. I'm not just the cook around here who runs a tight ship. I'm also Garrison's relationship guru. I sense early on when a romance is brewin'."

A red hue covered Jake's cheeks. "Mel and I are just friends."

Claire smirked. "Uh-huh. Right."

"We are!"

Claire walked through the swinging doors. "Whatever you say."

Jake looked at Anna for help.

She chuckled, shaking her head. "Give up, Jake."

He continued wiping the counter. "Hey, Anna?" he asked casually.

She inched the mug toward her mouth. "Yeah?"

"I was wondering...could, uh...could we go to church Sunday?"

She nearly choked. Slapping her chest, she tried rerouting the liquid. "Excuse me?"

He hunched over the counter, swirling the wet rag in an unproductive circular motion. "Can we go to church?"

Jake's willingness to spend Sunday morning in church with Garrison's All-American girl was sweet, but he was getting a little carried away.

"You don't have to try so hard to impress Melanie. She already likes you."

"I'm not doing it for her." His expression turned serious. "This for me."

That's when it hit Anna. His time spent at youth group had been more than just okay.

"Did something happen last night?"

His head drooped down. "Yeah... Sort of."

He didn't have to say another word. She already knew.

"When my parents were alive, I didn't go to church. I never thought about God or was really sure if He existed—"

"Until last night. Right?"

He nodded. "It sounds weird, but it felt like the right thing to do."

"By 'it' you mean?"

He paused. "I said a prayer. I got saved."

An unenthused, "Oh," slipped past Anna's lips.

Jake spoke about the evening with a play by play. "Going to church didn't sound like fun, but it was. Not just because of Melanie." He dipped his head and chuckled. "You know what I mean."

Anna nodded, pretending to be interested. Deep down, she didn't want to hear it.

"It was everything. The music was kinda like rock, only with Christian lyrics. And I really like Pastor Gill. He's cool, like one of the guys."

She forced a smile. "I'm glad you had a good time, Jake." She sipped her tea, hoping to end of the conversation.

"I'm still not sure what it all means or what I'm supposed to do now. But I'd like to find out. So, can we?"

"You mean, go to church? Sure, you can go if you want."

"What about you? Aren't you going too?"

"I don't think so, Jake. I haven't been to church in years."

His eyebrows scrunched together. "What does that have to do with anything?"

She suspected Pastor Gill put the church's newest believer on a recruiting mission to get her back to the faith. He'd already struck out, so why not let the kid take a swing? But Jake's spiritual awakening did nothing to revive hers.

"Look, you can go to church, to youth group, to every God function in Garrison until we leave. But *I'm not* going to church. Got it?"

His hands went up in surrender. "Yeah, I got it." Under his breath, he mumbled, "Just thought I'd ask."

He picked up the bucket, tossed the rag inside, and headed toward the kitchen but stopped before going through the swinging doors. He turned around. "Anna?"

She let out an irritated sigh. "No, Jake."

He set the bucket down. "It's not about church. I was wondering if..." His voice trailed off.

"What?"

He hesitated, staring at the floor. "Mel and some friends from youth group asked if I could go to the movies with them tonight. It's a group thing," he said, trying to reassure her. "I said I didn't have any money, but Mel said she would pay for me."

"How are you going to get there? The theater is in Muncie."

"Mrs. Thompson said she'll drop us off and pick us up. Then we're going to hang out at the diner."

Aside from the ignition incident, Jake had been playing by the rules. He showed up on time for work, he wanted to spend his free time in church with squeaky-clean teens, and perhaps the most surprising, his new-found faith. A night out at the movies with friends seemed like a reasonable reward.

"Sure, you can go. But I want you back by ten thirty, not a minute later. Okay?"

He smiled. "Thanks."

"Jake?"

"Yeah?"

Anna rummaged through her purse looking for her wallet. She pulled it out buried beneath a cosmetic bag and cell phone, unzipped it, and handed him thirty dollars.

"Pay for the lady." She thought about the pricey snacks at the concession stand and gave him an additional twenty. "And spring for some popcorn and soda."

His eyes widened. "Thanks, Anna." He folded the bills in half and shoved the money in his rear pants pocket.

She glanced at her watch. It was two o'clock. She had enough time to crank out a few more chapters before dinner. She downed the last gulp of tea, grabbed her purse, and said goodbye to Jake and Claire. She was making sure her wallet was back in her purse when she nearly ran into Carl Jenkins.

He stopped dead in his tracks. Removing his worn baseball cap, he gave a slight nod of a greeting. "Hello, Anna."

The muscles in her face tightened around the corners of her mouth, setting in a frown. "Carl," she responded in a cool tone.

He fumbled with his hat. "I heard you were back. I been meaning to stop by."

Her eyes shifted to his forearm. His tanned skin failed to hide a large scar. He covered the painful reminder with his hand.

Anna proceeded toward the exit, but he stopped her. "Can we talk? Just for a minute. Please?"

"I can't right now. I'm kind of busy."

Tears glazed over his eyes. "I've had this bottled up for eight years." He stepped closer. "Please, let me say what I need to say."

"Carl, it's done. It's over."

As Anna pushed the door open, his quivering voice made her stop. "I tried. I really tried to save her."

Images flashed before her like lightening, one after another of her helpless mother trapped in the car as consuming flames surrounded her.

She turned around. "Why didn't you call an ambulance?"

"There wasn't time. I just reacted."

She huffed, crossing her arms against her chest. "No, Carl. You had to play hero."

"Anna it wasn't–"

"She died because of you."

"No," he whispered, shaking his head. "It was too late. She was already gone."

"You don't know that!"

"Anna, I was there...you weren't."

How dare he!

The corner of her mouth trembled like wolf ready to devour dinner. She wanted to punch him, punch him hard and make him hurt the way he'd made her hurt. She got right in his face.

"Stay away from me. Do you hear me? I don't want to see you. I don't want to hear your voice. I mean it, Carl. Stay away from me."

She pushed the door open and stormed out of the diner.

Anna's legs felt like two steel beams as she ran down Mitner Road.

Blowing off her daily running regime for two months put her more out of shape than expected. The five extra pounds she'd gained before coming to Garrison and the few additional ones she'd packed on were contributing factors to her poor performance.

Sweat trickled down the sides of her face. The late afternoon humidity pushed her lungs to work twice as hard. If she didn't stop to catch her breath, she'd collapse right there on the side of the road.

Hunched over with her hands on her knees, she peered up at the cemetery.

She walked through the wrought iron arch and onto the burial grounds like a cautious trespasser on private property.

What made him think he could pull her out of a burning car?

It was his fault. Carl Jenkins was to blame. Her mother died because of him.

Anna ran out of the cemetery—harder and faster than her body allowed. No finish line to cross; she just ran. Her jaw ached from her clenched teeth, but she pushed through the pain with spurts of screams in between grunts of agony.

Her sneakers scuffled wildly against the loose stones. Her legs couldn't keep up with the sprint. She lost her footing and tripped over her own feet.

Her hands sprung out in front of her, instinctively shielding her chest from the inevitable fall. A loud thunk ensued when her body slapped belly first onto the gravel. Dust particles shot up in her face as she managed to keep it from scraping against the ground. Her hands and knees, however, were not spared.

She gasped for oxygen. Pools of blood covered her palms. She buried her face into the ground and sobbed. Not because she fell. Not because of the pain.

She curled into a ball on the side of the road bawling, wishing her mother would scoop her up like she did when she was a little girl, cradle her in her arms, kiss her boo-boos, and make the pain go away.

But her mother wasn't coming. She'd never come back again.

All Anna had was an open wound that would never heal.

Chapter Twenty-Six

Seated on the couch with the laptop resting on her thighs, Anna's fingers bounced from top to bottom and side to side on the keyboard. The quick movements weakened the elasticity of her bandages with every stretch. She stopped typing and turned her hands over. The edges of the wide Band-Aids covering her wounded palms peeled away from her skin.

Pulling off the adhesive, she stared at the exposed, raw flesh, then reattached the Band-Aids and resumed typing. Writing served as distraction from her run-in with Carl and unexpected visit to the cemetery.

Feeling the need for a cold drink, Anna saved her document and went to the kitchen to get the last can of Pepsi tucked in the back corner of the refrigerator. She grabbed the can off the top shelf and pulled back the aluminum tab. A curt snap, then a mist of soda sprayed out from the opened seal.

She normally avoided soft drinks. Then again, she had done quite a few anomalous things lately. Returning to Garrison. Bringing a law-breaking teen along for the trip. Going to her mother's eternal resting place. Why not add a Pepsi to the list?

Jake was the one in the house who drank soda but she doubted if he'd even care they ran out. He'd had more important things on his mind, like his group date with Melanie.

Anna chugged half the beverage in two large gulps, then returned to the couch and writing. There was a knock at the door. She took another quick gulp, set the can on the coffee table, and opened the door to see Melanie standing on the porch.

"Hi, Miss Sutton.

Anna held the screen door open. "Hi, Melanie, come in."

Melanie looked lovely in a sleeveless peach sundress and white sandals. She had on a touch more makeup than usual, particularly around her eyes, and her blond hair was pulled back in a curly ponytail.

"Jake," Anna called out. "Melanie's here!"

A frantic voice came from the bathroom. "I'll be right there!"

"Isn't that the girl's line?"

Melanie chuckled. "I think so."

Leaning in, Anna whispered, "He's been in there since he got home from the diner. An hour and a half! I don't even take that long to get ready."

"Me neither."

They both giggled and made small talk while waiting for Jake. He finally made his entrance, rendering Anna speechless.

Her mouth dropped. If she didn't know better, she would have thought he'd just finished a modeling shoot for a teen magazine. He'd traded in his overgrown hair for a longer version of a buzz cut with short spiky bangs. And his clothes! Anna didn't know his wardrobe consisted of anything but faded jeans and black T-shirts. But there he stood, wearing khaki shorts and a royal blue IZOD polo shirt. The head-to-toe transformation made him almost unrecognizable.

"Hi, Mel," he said, sticking his hands in his pockets. "You look great."

She smiled. "Thanks. So do you."

Still in awe, Anna chimed in. "When did you have time for a haircut?"

"Claire let me out early so I could go to Al's. He gave me a free haircut in exchange for cleaning up the barbershop every night next week."

"That was nice of him," Anna said.

"Yeah," he replied in a faraway tone. "It sure was."

Jake's mouth was moving, but his eyes didn't move a muscle. They stayed on Melanie.

Anna was beginning to feel invisible as the teens were lost in adoration of each other. "Well, you better get going. You don't want to be late."

Jake scooted around Melanie and held the door open for her.

"Bye, Miss Sutton." She waved as she passed by Jake.

"Bye. Have a good time. And Jake, don't forget. Ten thirty."

"Okay. Bye."

Anna stood behind the screen door watching Melanie and Jake walk down the rickety porch steps toward a tan Dodge Caravan with the engine running.

Helen Thompson rolled down the window, and Jake shook her hand before opening the passenger door for Melanie. She leaned out the window and called out, "Welcome home!"

Anna tilted her head up and smiled. "Thanks, Helen."

She stuck her hand out the window, waving goodbye as she backed out of the bumpy driveway.

Chapter Twenty-Seven

"How's the book coming?"

Anna shrugged her shoulders, taking a sip of tea from her mug. "All right, I guess."

Claire had made an unannounced visit to the cottage an hour after Jake and Melanie left for the movies. The two women ended up where they normally did—on the porch swing, a cup of coffee in Claire's hands and a cup of green tea in Anna's. She cherished their quiet evenings together. Spending time with Claire was as close as Anna was going to get to being with her mother.

"How much have you got done?"

"About ten chapters."

"Well, that sounds like a nice dent, especially since you've only been here a few weeks."

"I suppose," Anna replied, taking another sip.

Claire stared at Anna. Her unspoken concern blasted like a laser beam. She rested her coffee mug on her lap. "What's wrong, darlin'? And please don't say nothing because I know when something is wrong with you."

Anna turned to her and smiled. "Oh, yeah? What gives me away so that I know what not to do the next time?"

"Very funny. Ha ha," she said with a smirk. "Come on,

now, I'm serious. I don't like seeing you so...so..."

"What?"

"Lost, I guess. It's the only word that comes to mind."

Anna sighed. "It's my book. I'm finally on a roll, you know. I hit double-digit chapters. I should be happy, but something is missing. I can't put my finger on it. But if I stop now and try to figure it out, I'll never finish. I don't know, maybe I'm reading too much into it."

Claire rubbed her shoulder. "Ah, don't worry, hon. You'll figure it out. You're smart like that."

The sound of footsteps scuffing against the gravel driveway drew their attention to a silhouetted figure walking toward the porch in the darkness. "For someone who's so smart, you're actin' pretty stupid to me."

Anna instantly recognized the gruff voice of the petite woman.

"Why, Mavis Jenkins, what brings you out here on this fine evening?" Claire's voice dripped with sarcasm.

"I ain't here to chitchat with you, Claire."

"Then you're here for me," Anna said. "I suppose your husband told you about our little run-in at the diner?"

She stepped closer. The dim porch light revealed her scowl. "Yeah, *Carl* told me what happened."

"I figured he would. I wondered how long it was going take you to get here." She glanced at her watch. "I expected you hours ago, Mavis."

"You haven't changed a bit, Anna. Coming back, actin' all

high and mighty. You think you're something with that fancy college degree, living in a big city, working some fancy-schmancy job. To you, we're just a bunch of country bumpkins!"

"Settle down," Claire said, motioning with her hands.

Mavis's hysteria bounced off Anna like a rubber ball. She reminded her of one of those little dogs that yipped and barked a lot. All they were good for was making noise.

Anna swayed back and forth in the porch swing. "Are you done, Mavis?"

"That man has been grieving for years! Not once, *not once* did he get a thank you from you...you ungrateful brat."

Claire stood to her feet, ready to go on a verbal attack of her own when Anna grabbed her arm and forced her to sit back down. "Let her finish."

Mavis inched her way closer to the porch like a lioness on the prowl. Her hand landed on the railing. "Have ya ever seen someone die right in front of you?" She pointed to her head. "It messes with your mind *real good*. Ask Carl. Nightmare after nightmare after nightmare—"

"Mavis, that's enough," Claire said, scolding the dairy farmer's wife.

"I ain't done!" she yelled back. "Before you point that righteous finger of judgment, think about this, Anna... Maybe *you're* the one to blame for the accident."

"Mavis, I said that's enough!" Claire shouted, standing up. "You've said your piece, now go."

A satisfied smile stretched across her face. "You're right, Claire. I said exactly what I wanted to say. I feel so much better."

Mavis spun around and marched across the lawn and out of sight.

Claire looked at Anna with pity. "You okay, darlin'?"

She shrugged her shoulders. "Mavis is a nut. Always has been. Nothing she says fazes me." She took a sip of tea as an awkward silence hovered over them.

Claire sat beside Anna and sighed. "It's been real nice having Jake at the diner."

"He turned out to be a pretty good kid. But I can't take all the credit. I think Melanie's had something to do with it."

"They sure do make a cute couple." She hesitated before saying, "Ya know...he's been asking questions."

Anna stared at the bottom of her empty mug, circling the rim with the tip of her finger. "Is that right?"

"Don't you wanna know what he's been asking?"

"I'm sure it's nothing exciting," she said, waving her hand in front of her face. "Probably what I was like as a kid. Some embarrassing stuff he can use against me, things like that."

"You're not even close."

Anna stood up. "How about another cup of coffee?" she asked and went inside the cottage.

Claire followed her. "How about we finish our talk?"

Anna dumped the used tea bag into the trashcan and took a new one from the box on the counter. Her friend's relentless pursuit to get her to spill her guts was beginning to agitate her. But she reluctantly addressed the issue, hoping Claire would eventually drop the subject. "What did you tell him?"

"Enough. But not what he really wants to know," she said from the living room.

Anna didn't have the nerve to turn around and face Claire. She poured what was left of the hot water from the tea pot into the mug.

"He's gonna find out, Anna. I'm surprised he hasn't already. Small town like Garrison, all he has to do is ask anyone. Don't you think it'd be best coming from you?"

Dipping the fresh tea bag up and down, she replied, "He's fixated on Melanie Thompson, not me."

"Maybe he should know the truth. Maybe you'll finally get closure."

Anna spun around. "I can't believe we're discussing this!"

Claire went into the kitchen. Suddenly, Anna felt trapped—physically and emotionally. She never thought the woman she's known her whole life would be the one to force her to go back to the past.

"Anna, Lydia was more than my best friend. I loved her like she was my own flesh and blood. Her death was hard on me, too. I can't imagine what you must have been feeling." Gently, Claire placed her hand on her shoulder. "But, darlin', there came a time when I had to move on with my life. You do too."

"I moved on."

"No, you ran. There's a difference. And you've been running ever since."

"You're crazy!" Anna squeezed past her and went into the living room.

"No, I'm right. Weeks after she died, you shot out of Garrison faster than a rocket."

"I had to move. I had a job."

"Come on, Anna. You couldn't find something around here? You wanted change and that's what you got. Everything changed about you. Heck, even the way you talk changed."

"What's wrong with the way I talk?"

"You buried your accent. Are you that ashamed to let folks know where you come from? Weren't you good enough for those big city folks?"

"I thought you were on my side. You're beginning to sound like Mavis."

"This isn't about sides. This is about you running away. Running from me, from relationships, and more importantly, running from God."

Anna arms shot up in the air. "Don't bring *Him* into this!"

"*He* is what this whole thing is about. You can't handle blaming yourself, so it's easier to blame God."

Anna folded her arms across her chest. "So, you think Mavis is right? You think it's my fault that Momma died."

Claire sighed. Her head lowered along with her voice.

"No, darlin', I don't. But deep down, you do… And it's killing you."

A tear ran down Anna's face.

"Anna, God can take all that pain, all that guilt away if you just let Him. Open up your heart and let Him back in."

Every time Claire said *God*, the volcano inside Anna got closer to erupting until she couldn't take it anymore.

"I trusted Him my whole life! What did He do for me in return? He took Momma away from me. Why didn't He protect her? He just let her die!"

Claire wrapped her arms around Anna. "I don't know, sweetie. I don't have an answer to why. But I know He still loves you, and He misses you."

"Well, I don't miss Him." She broke away from her embrace, fiercely wiping away tears. "I hate Him."

"You don't mean that."

"Yes, Claire, I do. Every word of it."

"Your momma raised you better. She'd be ashamed to hear you talk like this. I know I am."

Her words pierced Anna's heart like a knife.

Claire left the cottage, letting the screen door slam shut behind her.

Chapter Twenty Eight

The theater lights faded as the group of six teens walked up the steep staircase. The first of several lengthy movie previews appeared on the big screen.

Jake watched Liv grab Melanie's arm and whisper in her friend's ear. Liv smiled and winked before tossing a popcorn kernel from her bucket into her mouth. She continued walking up the staircase with Emma, Nick, and Shane following her to the top row of seats below a beam of light coming from the film projector.

Melanie pointed to an empty row. "Is this okay?"

"Sure," Jake replied, following her to the middle seats.

Holding the popcorn, he stared at the large bucket on his lap. "Would you like some?" he asked, shifting it closer to her.

She smiled. "Sure, thanks." Her delicate hand reached into the heap of buttery popcorn. One by one she softly chewed the kernels before taking a sip of her soda. "I love movie theater popcorn. But I can't get it to taste like this at home."

Jake reached into the bucket and took a handful of popcorn. "I know what you mean."

He wondered if the rest of the group was watching them

instead of the big screen. Turning his head, looking casually around the theater, he saw Nick give him a thumbs-up while the girls smiled and giggled.

Yep, they were watching.

Melanie reached over the armrest and helped herself to more popcorn. Jake kept the bucket as close to the middle of them as possible. He didn't want her to think he was hogging it.

The previews ended, and the movie finally began. The girls had picked a chick flick, but Jake didn't care. If it meant watching cartoons just to spend time with Melanie, he would have gladly done it, and he would've loved every minute of it.

She was the most beautiful girl he had ever seen. Inside and out. Her golden blond ponytail fell over her shoulder like a wavy waterfall. Her blue eyes made him smile the instant she looked in his direction. And he loved the way her front teeth tugged on her rosy pink bottom lip when she was at a loss for words.

As if she'd somehow heard his thoughts, Melanie looked at Jake. She said nothing, only smiled.

The teens turned their attention to the screen. Jake watched Melanie out of the corner of his eye as she chuckled at humorous scenes and smiled sweetly during the kissing scenes. He debated whether or not to hold her hand. Accepting his affection would make his night. Rejecting it would devastate him, but at least he wouldn't have to wonder how she felt. He'd know.

Everything logical inside his brain screamed *don't do it.* Everything hopeful whispered for him to go for it. So, he did. He reached over the armrest but lost his nerve and pulled back. Grabbing her hand as if he owned her seemed rude. Melanie was classy. She deserved more. She deserved better.

While her hands were loosely folded on her lap, Jake mustered up enough courage to try again. He lifted his hand slowly, like a magician conducting a levitating trick, then settled it gently on top of hers. Her skin was just as soft as the day she'd introduced herself to him at the diner.

He glanced at her, anxious to see her reaction. For a brief moment, time froze. Then a smile eased across her face. Without making eye contact, she turned her hand up, intertwined her fingers with his, and gently squeezed his hand. Just when Jake thought the night couldn't get any better, Melanie leaned over and rested her head on his shoulder.

Yep, she liked him. She really liked him.

Sitting at the kitchen table, Anna stared at the computer screen in a hopeless attempt to write another chapter. It was no use. She couldn't jot down a message on a Post-it Note let alone put together a chapter.

Her argument with Claire played out in her mind like a gruesome movie scene stuck on repeat. She cringed every time she heard her say she was ashamed of her.

Anna had lost her mother. She couldn't lose Claire too.

A face-to-face apology was in order, but Jake was due back from the movies in less than an hour. She didn't want him coming home to an empty house.

The kitchen chair squeaked against the wooden floor as she slid back. She picked up the phone receiver and slowly dialed Claire's number, taking big pauses in between each numeral until she got to the last one. But her finger wouldn't pull down the last digit and she hung up.

Walking back to the kitchen, Anna closed the lid to the laptop and went to bed.

Chapter Twenty Nine

After the movie, Melanie's mom dropped the teens off at the diner. After a late-night feeding frenzy on French fries and milkshakes, the group split up. Nick and Shane went home while the girls and Jake walked to the cottage.

Emma and Liv waited for Melanie at the end of driveway as she and Jake headed toward the porch. The wooden planks squeaked with each step they took. The dim porch light gave off enough illumination for him to stare at her. He'd barely let go of her hand since the movies.

"I had a great time tonight," she said.

"Me too." He stepped closer and took her other hand in his. As he leaned down to kiss her, Melanie met him halfway. Finally, his lips met hers. A shiver of excitement sent the hairs on his arms straight up. He wanted to be close to her, as close as he could get. He let go of her hands and slid his arms around her tiny waist, just as her arms found their way around his neck. Their first kiss was just as he'd imagined it would be.

Locked in an embrace, Melanie rested her head against Jake's chest. The smell of her hair reminded him of a strawberry patch.

She pulled back to see his face. Her blue eyes filled with

sadness, glossed over as if she was ready to cry. "I'm gonna miss you, Jake. I mean, when ya leave Garrison."

He pushed away a strand of her hair that had fallen across her forehead. "Why are you saying goodbye already? Summer isn't over. We still have a lot of time left." He stooped down, giving her another kiss.

She smiled. "You're right."

Jake pulled her toward him and hugged her.

"I could stay here all night. But I better get going," she said.

"Yeah, I don't want you to miss your curfew." Bending down, he gave her another kiss, then forced himself to let go of her.

Halfway down the squeaky steps, she turned around and flashed him a smile. "Good night."

"Night, Mel."

He watched her saunter down the gravel driveway and down the road until she and her friends were out of sight.

Standing on the porch, he thought about how much he'd hated the idea of coming to Garrison. He'd hated the diner, and he'd hated Anna. When he left Buffalo, he thought his summer was ruined. Shot to bits.

But the small Indiana town turned out to be a place he wanted to stay in, all because a girl named Melanie Thompson came into his life, and he was so thankful she had.

She'd only been gone two minutes and he already missed

her. He walked inside the cottage with a goofy smile still plastered on his face, expecting Anna to be on the couch working on her book.

His footsteps got lighter and quieter as he approached her bedroom. He peeked his head around the open door. She was in bed, tossing and turning in her sleep.

Tiptoeing back into the living room, he glanced at her laptop on the kitchen table. Cranking his neck around to make sure she wasn't behind him, he quietly pulled out a chair and sat down at the table. He opened the computer lid and pressed the start button. Once it booted up, he went to Google and typed *Indianapolis Star.*

At the newspaper's homepage, he searched for Lydia Sutton. It had been eight years since her death, and he wasn't sure how long newspapers kept articles online. But it was worth a shot.

A handful of matches appeared on the screen. Scrolling down the page, the headline "Crash Kills Garrison Diner Owner" caught his eye.

This has to be it.

He clicked on the link. The article appeared with a picture of the accident scene and a photograph of Lydia.

In a low whisper, he read the article.

"A one-car crash killed a Garrison restaurant owner late Tuesday night. Lydia Sutton, 42, of Garrison, was pronounced dead at the scene. Police say Sutton lost control of the car she was driving on County Road, then smashed into a tree,

causing the vehicle to burst into flames."

Jake cringed, imagining her being trapped inside a burning car. He continued reading.

"Sutton was co-owner of Claire's Diner and is survived by one daughter, Anna."

Jake had wanted to know how Lydia died. Now that he did, he wished he hadn't snooped. He understood why it was so hard for anyone close to her to talk about what happened. He clicked out of the website and turned off the computer.

It was going to be a long night.

Chapter Thirty

The aroma of hotcakes and sausage made its way to Anna's bedroom, poking at her nose and waking her up from a deep sleep. The tantalizing smell combined with the sound of clanging pans and dishes tricked her into thinking she was at the diner.

Squinting at the bright light coming through her window, the morning sun confirmed she was indeed in bed at the cottage.

Still groggy and somewhat confused, she grabbed her robe from the bedpost. The silky garment covered her plaid pajama shorts and Channel 3 News T-shirt. She staggered out of the bedroom barefoot to the kitchen where Jake was cooking breakfast.

Anna watched in awe as he stood in front of the stove turning over sausage links in a cast iron skillet and flipping over two rows of hotcakes on an electric griddle with ease.

"You made breakfast?" she asked.

"Hey, you're finally up," he replied, turning off the burner.

Finally? How late was it?

She looked at the clock. Eight forty-five. Then she remembered it was Saturday, which explained why Jake was at the cottage instead of the diner.

He lifted a hotcake high enough with a spatula to check the bottom. Both sides were golden brown. He scooped them off the griddle one at a time and slid three of them on each plate.

Anna sat down at the kitchen table. A stick of butter and a bottle of maple syrup were placed in the center. He hadn't forgotten anything, not even the utensils and napkins at both place settings. Claire had taught him well.

With a plate in each hand, he set his dish down then hers, proudly announcing, "Pancakes, or as you call them, hotcakes, sausage, and..."

He went to the counter and returned holding a mug. "Green tea with a slice of lemon."

She stared at him as if he were a stranger as she took the mug.

He sat down next to her, cut off a chunk of butter with his knife, and swirled it back and forth on the warm hotcakes before dousing them in maple syrup.

"Why did you do all this?" Anna asked.

He shrugged his shoulders. "Just felt like it."

Yeah, right! A teenager getting up early on a Saturday to make breakfast! She wasn't buying it.

"What did you do?" Suspicion coated her tone.

He scrunched his face. "Huh?"

"What did you do?" she repeated, raising her voice. "What happened?"

"Nothing."

"Then what is this all about," she said, pointing the scrumptious breakfast.

He set the knife against the edge of the plate. "I thought you had more faith in me than that."

Ouch, that hurt.

"But if you really need to know, I just wanted to do something nice for you. That's it."

Anna's face softened to the point of shame. She felt like such a jerk for assuming the worst. "Jake, I'm sorry. I shouldn't have accused you of anything. It was really nice of you to do all this. I mean it, really. Thanks."

"Ahh, it's okay. I guess I would've thought something was up too if I were you. I'm here because I screwed up."

For the first time since they arrived in Garrison, Jake expressed remorse for his part in the robbery. Anna leaned over and put her hand on top of his. His brown eyes met hers. A sad, faraway look stared back at her.

"We all make mistakes," she said. "It's learning from them that's important."

He smiled. "Yeah, I guess you're right."

She patted his hand, trying to lighten the mood. "Of course, I am." She rubbed her hands together with great anticipation. "Enough talking, let's eat!"

"Sounds good. I'll pray."

Jake had gone out of his way to do something nice. The least Anna could do was go along with a blessing. Hesitantly, she clasped her hands together.

Closing his eyes, Jake bowed his head and prayed out loud. "Thank you, Lord, for the food. Thank you that it will help our bodies. And thank you we can enjoy a meal together. Amen."

A stuttered "Amen" slipped past her lips. His simple prayer was to the point, what she expected from a novice Christian. Not that she had any right to critique his prayer life. She hadn't said a single prayer in eight years.

Anna smeared a thick coat of butter across the hotcakes and drizzled maple syrup over them. Tearing off a chunk with her fork, she shoved a piece into her mouth. Her taste buds were pleasantly surprised at how good the fluffy hotcakes turned out.

"This is delicious," she said, unable to wait until swallowing. Covering her mouth with her hand, she finished chewing. "Who taught you to make hotcakes?"

Jake stared at his plate, slowly twisting his fork from side to side. In a solemn tone he replied, "Mom made them every Saturday morning." A bittersweet smile spread across his face. "It was kinda like a tradition."

Anna remained quiet, hoping he'd reveal more about their relationship.

"She called me her little assistant." He chuckled at the title. "I was in charge of handing her the ingredients and stirring the batter. Sometimes she let me pour it on the griddle. She made me feel important. But I guess moms are supposed to do that."

191

His short-lived bond with his mother made Anna think of Lydia. She'd been her biggest cheerleader, always making her feel like she could do anything no matter how the odds were stacked.

Jake cut a triangular piece of hotcake with his fork. Before he popped it into his mouth, she blurted out, "Your mom would be proud of you, and not just because of the hotcakes."

Anna didn't have to explain what she meant. It was clear from the look on his face he already knew.

They finished breakfast in silence. Anna scraped every crumb off her plate, as did Jake. The tea had time to cool off so the temperature was just right.

"Ahh. Perfect," she said after taking a sip.

She insisted on doing the dishes and was at the sink when Jake announced out of the blue, "I know what happened to your mom."

The plate she was rinsing nearly slipped from her grasp.

She turned off the faucet, placed the dish in the rack, and reached for a towel to dry her hands. She was naive to think she'd get through the whole summer without him finding out the truth. Garrison was a small town. It had only been a matter of time before someone spilled the beans.

"Melanie told you?" she asked, placing the towel over the door handle on the oven to dry.

He shook his head. "I went on your laptop and found an article online. Are you mad?"

"No, Jake, I'm not. Actually, I'm relieved. I didn't think I would be, but I am." She was ready to tell him everything and sat down at the table. "I suppose you're wondering how it happened?"

He sat down next to her. "Well...yeah. Sort of."

Anna's cup of tea was still on the table. She took a sip to moisten her dry throat. It was lukewarm, on the verge of cold, but it didn't matter.

"My senior year of college, I met a guy named Austin Porter. All the girls were crazy about him." She raised her hand with a guilty grin. "Including me. He'd strut through the student union with his entourage. You'd think he was a celeb by the way people huddled around him. Guys thought he was cool. Girls chased after him like puppy dogs."

She paused to gather her thoughts.

"He had a reputation. Guys like that always do. He'd go out with a girl for a while, get what he wanted, then dump her." She raised her eyebrows. "Know what I mean?"

He gave a crooked smile.

Anna wrung her sweaty hands as Jake listened to her spill her guts.

"We were at a party when he finally noticed me. He said he'd been wanting to talk to me all semester. We started dating and he said all the right things. Told me how special I was, that he'd never felt the way he did about a girl until me. All the sappy stuff girls can't get enough of." She grinned. "He made me feel I was some kind of miracle that

193

changed his life. I believed what we had was real."

She let out a sarcastic snort. "It was all bull. Every word of it. But I was young and stupid. My Spidey-senses weren't as sharp as they are now. Austin was as shallow as they come. He was just a good-looking guy with a smile that made me melt who gave me some attention."

Anna sighed, wanting to stop and hoping Jake would suggest she'd do so. But he didn't. How could he? She had set an intriguing table.

"I should've known better. Momma did. She loathed him, and if you knew Momma, you would've known it took a lot for her to feel that way about another human being. But she couldn't stand Austin. The way he groped me in front of her, how he rudely addressed her by her first name. Not to mention the rumor mill swirling when he was spotted in town drunk. More than once."

"One night, it all came to a head. Momma and I got into a huge fight. She told me to stop seeing him, and I refused. But before I knew it, dumping Austin was the least of my worries."

Jake's eyebrows scrunched together. "What do you mean?"

Anna took a sip of tea and stared down at the cup. "Before Momma died, I found out about my real father."

"I can't believe ya lied to me!"

Anna stood in front of Lydia with her clenched fists glued to her side. She didn't know what made her madder: her mother's fabrication or the truth itself. Finding out she was the result of a one-night stand came as the shock of her life. Every part of her parents' short-lived marriage was made up, like scenes from a fiction book. There was no romantic elopement. No celebratory dinner when Lydia announced she was having a baby. No tragic car accident that took his life two months before Anna was born. The doting husband and proud father-to-be never existed. Her mother rarely mentioned him, and now she knew why.

Lydia's brown eyes pleaded for understanding. "I did it to protect you, Anna."

"Protect me?" she repeated in disgust. "Lying about who I am is your way of protecting me?"

No explanation made Anna disregard why Lydia did what she did. The one person she completed trusted had betrayed her for twenty-two years. It felt like a knife stabbing her over and over.

Tears coated Lydia's eyes. "I kept the truth from you because I thought that was best at the time."

Anna didn't want to hear more excuses. She wanted answers.

"What's his name?"

Lydia's voice quivered. "W-what?"

"My father. You know, the one who's alive. What's his real name?"

Lydia was silent.

"Momma? I deserve to know my father's name!"

"Anna, it's not important."

Her response knocked the wind out of Anna, as if someone hauled off and punched her in the stomach.

"Not important? What's the matter with you? I want to know his name, and I want to know right now!"

Lydia hung her head. "Andrew Prescott," she mumbled.

"I suppose ya lied about him being a lawyer too."

"No," she said quickly, as if it offered her some redemption. "That's true. He's a lawyer in Chicago."

Anna folded her arms across her chest. "Why, Momma? Why'd you keep him from me?"

"If I told you, you'd wanna meet him."

"What's wrong with that?"

"Anna." She stopped.

"What, Momma? What else aren't you telling me?"

Lydia's hand covered her mouth. She looked like she was going to vomit. "Your father was married when I met him."

Anna's jaw dropped. "What?"

"Please, don't make me say it again."

Anna's hands flew up in the air. "You had an affair with a married man? Well, this just gets better and better."

"I didn't know. He wasn't wearing a wedding ring, and I didn't think to ask."

Anna snorted. "Why would you? You were too busy doing *other* things."

"You watch your tone, young lady." Lydia's voice turned firm.

Anna ran her fingers through her hair and blew a heavy sigh. Her mother had slept with a man she barely knew, a man promised to another woman. Her virtuous image was tarnished. The woman Anna once revered and looked up to had become unrecognizable.

No, this isn't happening.

It couldn't be happening. That kind of thing didn't happen in Garrison.

Oh no.

Everyone who knew Lydia had to know about the affair. How many times had people looked at Anna and thought, *there's Lydia's illegitimate kid?*

She closed her eyes. She couldn't stand to look at her mother or be in the same room with her. As she walked away, Lydia grabbed her wrist and gripped it tightly. "Sweetheart," she pleaded, "as much as this hurts me to say, you need to hear it...all of it."

Anna turned around and stared with contempt.

"After you were born, I tracked down your father. I felt I owed it to him to let him know he had a beautiful daughter." She sniffled, fighting to hold back tears on the brink of falling down her pale, silky skin.

With pity in her eyes, she continued. "But your father

wasn't the same man I fell in love with. He was cold. Distant. He didn't have feelings for me like I thought he did." She grabbed Anna's other wrist. "He said he wanted nothing to do with me or you. He said he wasn't gonna let a fling with a hick ruin his marriage and his reputation. He told me if I ever contacted him again, he'd make life miserable for me...and you. I was young and scared. Andrew was a lawyer from a big city, probably with connections and money. Who knows what he was capable of?"

Glaring at her mother, Anna's anger spread in her heart like a wildfire. "Why should I believe you? Ya lied to me my whole life. You're still lying to me!"

"Anna, I'm not ly—"

"You'll say anything to make him look bad and you like the poor victim."

She pulled away from her, went into her bedroom, and slammed the door. She could hear her mother's cries. But no matter how many tears were shed, it didn't excuse what she did. It didn't change the fact that she had a father all along. And it didn't change what she was about to do.

"I need you to take me to Chicago. Tonight."

"The Windy City? Sure thing, babe. We'll cozy up in a nice motel along the way."

In Anna's rage, she would've agreed to a crime spree if it meant getting to Chicago.

"Fine. Pick me up in twenty minutes." She ended the call and tossed her cell phone into her purse.

She pulled out a suitcase from the closet and tossed it on the bed. The howling wind sent her attention to the bedroom window. She pulled back the curtain. The dark sky guaranteed a storm was on the way.

She unzipped the suitcase and threw random articles of clothing inside without much concern to match the tops to the bottoms. Her hasty packing job was almost done. She looked at her watch. Austin would be there soon. She didn't want to keep him waiting or give her mother a chance to try and talk her out of leaving.

Pushing down on the pile, Anna made room for a few more shirts when she realized she didn't know what Andrew looked look. She didn't have a picture, and she wasn't going to ask her mother for a description, that was for certain.

The Internet—of course!

A wave of relief swept away her panic. *Thank God for technology.*

Her basic flip phone didn't have web access. She made a mental note to head to the nearest library first thing in the morning to start her research.

Glancing out the window, she watched the top of trees sway fiercely from side to side. From the looks of it, the weather was going to be a hinderance. But no silly little windstorm would stop her from finding Andrew Prescott.

She imagined the shock on his face after introducing herself. Understandably so. Perhaps he would even be speechless at the sight of his daughter, his first-born child all grown up.

His first-born?

Chances are he had children with his wife. That meant Anna had siblings. She smiled at the thought of a brother or sister, especially a sister. Being an only child was lonely at times. No one to confide in. No one to get in trouble with. No one to go on double-dates with. Sure, she had friends from school and church, but college took them in different directions. A sibling relationship meant a biological bond that miles could not break.

Anna was determined more than ever to find Andrew and prove her mother wrong.

She pushed down on the heap of clothes in the suitcase when a bright light shone in the window. Tires squealed as a black Camaro made a sharp turn into the driveway. Austin was there.

Anna zipped the suitcase shut and grabbed her purse. She dug through the sack for her wallet. There was fifty dollars and a handful of coins inside, plus her credit card in case of an emergency. She shoved the wallet back into the purse, flung it over her shoulder, and picked up the suitcase.

Out in the driveway, Austin honked the car horn twice.

She confidently opened her bedroom door and headed toward the small entryway where Lydia was standing. Her eyes were puffy. She sniffled, using a crumpled tissue to wipe her red nose.

When she noticed the suitcase, her countenance changed. As if she already knew the answer, she asked the question anyway. "Where ya going?"

The weight from the suitcase sent Anna's purse sliding down her arm. She heaved the falling strap up back on her shoulder and replied, "Chicago," in a stone-cold tone.

Lydia stepped in front of Anna. "Don't go. Please, listen to me, you'll regret it." Her voice crackled. "Trust me."

A sarcastic chuckle escaped past Anna's lips. "You want *me* to trust *you* after all those lies? You gotta be kidding."

"The truth about your father is the *only* thing I ever kept from you. I never lied about anything else. Anna, I did—"

"Yeah, yeah, I know," she said, cutting her off. "You did what ya thought was best at the time. But guess what, Momma? You were wrong. What ya thought was best for me turned out to be a big mistake." She paused, then muttered, "Just like me."

Lydia grabbed her arms. "Don't ever say that again. Ya hear me? Anna, I never, ever thought of you as a mistake. God blessed me with a beautiful, intelligent daughter. I'm so proud of the woman you are. You're the best thing that ever happened to me."

A layer of anger melted away at her heartfelt speech. Anna wanted their fight to end. She wanted her relationship with her mother—her best friend—to go back to the way it was. But then she thought about Andrew. He'd missed out on years of birthdays and holidays. Maybe he didn't want anything to do with them because he was scared. His infidelity could've ended his marriage. But in time, he would've come around. He would have wanted to meet her; she was convinced of it. They could have had a real father-daughter relationship. Phone calls, letters, and summers in Chicago. It was possible.

The more Anna thought about what she'd missed with Andrew, the angrier she became at her mother. She squirmed free from her grasp.

Lydia slid her body against the door.

"Momma, I have to go."

"No, you don't."

"Yes, I do."

Anna turned and tugged on the doorknob. That's when her mother snapped.

"Anna Marie Sutton, I forbid you to go!"

"You can't stop me! I'm an adult, and I make my own decisions!" she screamed back, whipping the door open.

"Get back here!"

"No!" Anna shouted, slamming the front door hard enough the hinges rattled.

She took off running down the porch steps, squinting as

the wind pushed against her face. Her suitcase thumped back and forth against her leg.

Austin stayed planted behind the wheel of his precious Camaro, offering little assistance as he reached across the front seat to open the passenger door a mere inch.

She fumbled with her suitcase while trying to open the door. Once inside the sports car, she chucked the luggage in the backseat.

"Nice hair." He looked her up and down. "Makes you look pretty hot the way it's all messed up."

She shot him a half-hearted smile as she pushed away strands of hair plastered across her face. Anna felt anything but hot. His naughty grimace implied one thing—he wanted to get her to the nearest motel.

She looked back at the house. Lydia stood on the porch, looking miserable. "Come on, let's get outta here."

His eyebrows jerked up. "Gladly." He threw the car in reverse and floored it, peeling out of the driveway.

In a blink, the house was out of sight. The farther they drove, the more Anna knew distance from her mother was in her best interest. Lydia needed time to cool off, and she needed time to get to know her father. After a few days, life could start getting back to normal. It would be a new normal, but one she was ready to embrace.

But Anna had been wrong. Dead wrong.

Chapter Thirty One

"Every time I left the house, I told Momma I loved her. I didn't that night. It's something that still haunts me to this day."

Anna gulped the last bit of tea, now officially cold. She hated herself for the way she'd acted. Her mother's confession was the hardest thing she'd ever had to admit. Lydia needed her daughter's understanding and forgiveness. Anna gave her neither.

She looked at Jake and debated whether or not to continue. The warmth in his eyes gave her the assurance that he hadn't judged her so far and wasn't going to no matter what she said.

"I made two mistakes that night. Leaving Momma the way I did and turning to Austin Porter for help."

"Why? What happened?" Jake asked.

The volume of Anna's voice lowered. "He lived up to his reputation."

Austin pulled the Camaro into the parking lot of a motel off Interstate 90. Anna tried convincing him to keep driving until they reached Chicago. She even offered to take over at the wheel, but he insisted they call it a night.

She got her suitcase and reluctantly followed him to the motel office. The flashing, pink neon sign read "VACANCY" in the window adding a layer of dinginess to the low-class establishment.

A musty stench greeted her senses when they approached the front desk. A man with his back to them sat in a rickety brown chair while watching an old black and white movie on a thirteen-inch television set. Austin tapped the silver bell on the counter once to get his attention.

"Yeah?" the man said in a gruff voice.

Austin glanced at Anna, grinning. "We'll take your best room for the night."

The heavy-set man stood up sporting a faded yellow T-shirt two sizes too small. He cleared his throat and sniffed. "Twenty-two dollars."

Austin handed him the money in exchange for the key.

The peevish cashier was very matter-of-fact. "Room 9," he said, pointing straight ahead. "Head out the door and swing left. Ice machine is outside next to Room 5. Check out is at eleven. No continental breakfast. Enjoy your stay."

He plopped back down in the chair and continued watching the movie.

Austin held up the key and raised his eyebrows. "Let's go."

The same funky smell in the office lingered throughout

room 9. Austin tossed his duffle bag on the floor. He nodded his head. "Yeah, this'll do."

Anna stared at the chipped panel walls. The stained carpet precluded her from setting down her purse and suitcase. She resorted to a wobbly, circular table. Running a finger through a thick layer of dust, it was safe to assume the motel didn't have a cleaning service. If it did, they were doing a lousy job.

"A little overpriced, don't ya think?"

"Ahh, it's not bad." He did a swan dive onto the bed. The springs squeaked as he bounced up and down on the mattress. From the look of the gaudy pink and yellow bedspread, she doubted it had ever seen the inside of a washing machine.

Austin patted the ugly comforter. "Bed is comfy. Try it out."

Anna held her breath, paralyzed with fear.

"Com'on over," he said with a sexy smile.

She sat on the edge of the bed with her back to him. She couldn't look him in the face. She'd been in similar situations with her boyfriend but always managed to ward off his advances. Not this time. She was hundreds of miles away from home without a car. Anna was stranded.

Austin's hand rubbed up and down her arm. He scooted closer. Pushing her hair aside, he covered the nape of her neck in soft, gentle kisses. If her heart raced any faster, it would explode.

She jumped off the bed. "I'll be right back," she blurted out, heading to the bathroom. "It was a long trip."

She shut the door.

Think, Anna, think!

She flipped the light switch and wished she hadn't. She pulled back the flimsy shower curtain to find mold along the top edge. Brown soap scum circled the inside of the tub. "Yuck." Her stomach turned at the thought of sleeping in the unsanitary bathroom.

She rinsed her hands under the faucet and patted her flushed cheeks with cool water when she heard her phone ring. She wiped her face on her sleeve and opened the door.

Austin held up the phone. "That's enough interruptions for one night." He put the ringer on silent and tossed the gadget into her purse.

Anna rushed toward him. "I better check–"

Cupping her face in his hands, he silenced her with his lips and led her to the foot of the bed. He pressed his weight against her. She lost her balance and landed backward on the mattress. He crawled on top of her and held her wrists while passionately kissing her. If there was one thing Austin was good at, it was kissing. The moment his lips touched hers, she lost all clarity.

His mouth moved to her neck and up to her ear. He whispered, "I love you."

What? Anna pushed him off her enough to see his face. "What did you just say?"

"You heard me," he said, tracing her lips with his finger. A devilish grin spread across his face. "But if you want me to say it again, I will. I love you, Anna."

The three words she'd been waiting to hear rendered her speechless. She had the perfect opportunity to finally tell Austin she felt the same way. But the words refused to come out. They were loud and clear in her head. She stammered and stuttered like a fool before he picked up where he left off, kissing her with an intensity unlike she'd ever experienced.

What she was about to do went against everything she held to be true. She knew it was wrong, but that night, she needed someone not only tell her they loved her, she needed someone to show her they loved her.

After weeks of resisting Austin Porter's sexual advances, Anna finally gave in.

Anna watched the red numbers on the alarm clock switch from 2:59 to 3:00.

Austin's rhythmic snore wasn't the only thing keeping her awake. Lying on his stomach, shirtless in his boxer shorts, his rock-hard physique did absolutely nothing to excite her.

Picking up his arm draped across her torso, she let it flop on the scuzzy mattress as she slid out to use the bathroom.

He squirmed in his sleep, rubbing his head side to side into the pillow and continued snoring.

Hunched over the grime-filled sink, Anna washed her hands with a cruddy bar of soap. She caught a glimpse of her reflection in the mirror. She looked different. She didn't think she would, but she did.

Disappointment glared back at her. She had become her mother. She'd followed in her footsteps. She'd slept with a man she wasn't married to.

Turning her head away in shame, she scrubbed her hands so hard, they turned a red hue. It wasn't enough. She rinsed them with hot water, as hot as she could get it. But no amount of soap or steaming water made her feel clean. She turned off the faucets and dried her hands.

If she couldn't look at herself in the mirror without feeling disgrace, how could God look at her? How could He ever love her?

Anna felt like a piece of glass teetering on the edge of an unsteady table, ready to fall and shatter into a million pieces.

The rusty hinges on the bathroom door let out a prolonged squeak. Standing in the doorway, she stared at Austin. She was an emotional wreck after learning the truth about her mother and father. She was vulnerable and weak—a combination he used to his advantage.

Why didn't I say no?

Tears stung her eyes as. She'd ruined a once-in-a lifetime

moment meant to be pure. A moment for someone special who truly loved her. She had been saving herself for her husband on their wedding night, not her boyfriend in a sleazy motel off Interstate 90.

Forever, Austin Porter would be linked to her.

Anna had lost more than her virginity. She'd lost a part of herself.

Chapter Thirty-Two

"We never made it to Chicago," Anna said, staring at the bottom of her cup. "The next morning, there was a message on my phone from Claire letting me know about Momma. I cried the whole way home."

"Austin acted as if nothing happened. He was useless. He didn't even have the decency to show up to the funeral, not that it mattered. A few days later, one of his buddies told me he didn't want to see me anymore. The coward didn't even have the guts to break up with me in person."

Jake leaned forward, immersed in her story. "Did you meet ever meet your dad?"

Her voice crackled. "Yes."

The slow elevator ride to the twelfth floor stopped multiple times to let people get on and off. Confined in a space the size of a tiny bathroom, standing shoulder to shoulder with strangers, made Anna claustrophobic. Then there was the dreaded eye contact and awkward smiles. But the ride was better than walking twelve floors in her new high heels.

A dinging sound indicated another stop. Gazing up at the row of numbered circles above the door, twelve was lit up. Finally, she'd reached her destination. Her hands ran over her pink silk top and black skirt, smoothing out any wrinkles. She wanted to look her best.

The double doors opened. She adjusted her purse strap and went to the semi-circle desk where a middle-aged woman sat fervently typing on her computer. A large sign on the wall behind her read "Martin, Hertz, and Prescott." The brass nameplate on the edge of her desk simply read, "RECEPTION."

"Good morning."

The brunette turned her attention away from the screen and greeted Anna with a professional smile. "May I help you?"

"Yes, I'm here to see Andrew Prescott."

"Your name, please?"

"Anna Sutton."

The woman clicked the calendar document and scrolled down the screen. "I don't see your name. Do you have an appointment?"

"No, ma'am, I don't. It's a last-minute meeting."

"I'm sorry. Mr. Prescott goes by appointment only. Would you like to schedule one now?"

"When is he available?"

"Let's see here," she said, mumbling to herself scanning the electronic calendar. She shook her head. "I'm afraid he's booked for a while." She glanced up with an apologetic smile. "It'll be four weeks."

Four weeks! I can't wait four weeks. I've already waited twenty-two years! I need to see my father!

Anna politely pleaded her case, hoping the receptionist would help her out. "Ma'am, I know ya got a job to do, and I don't mean to be difficult. But I *need* to see Mr. Prescott today. I came all the way from Indiana. Please, ma'am...it's urgent."

Whether it was the desperation in her eyes or the pathetic way she said "urgent," something swayed the receptionist.

"You're in luck, you caught me on a good day." She picked up the receiver. "I'll see what I can do, but I can't guarantee anything. What's your name again?"

"Anna Sutton. From Garrison, Indiana."

The receptionist dialed a three-digit extension.

Anna threw in, "Tell him I'm Lydia's daughter."

She nodded, signaling she understood. He must have been at his desk because after one ring the receptionist started talking. "Mr. Prescott, I have a young lady here to see you, but she doesn't have an appointment." The faint sound of a garbled voice could be heard on the other end of the receiver. "I know, Mr. Prescott, I told her, but she says it's urgent that she sees you."

A pause. The receptionist shot a look as if she was rooting for her. "Anna Sutton from Garrison, Indiana."

Another pause. "Yes, Sutton. She told me to tell you she's Lydia's daughter."

Either her mother's name shocked him or sent him searching his memory bank. Anna, along with the receptionist, eagerly waited for a reply.

She looked her up and down. "Yes, early twenties" she said, lowering the volume of her voice. "I'll let her know." She hung up the phone. "Mr. Prescott will be with you in a moment."

The receptionist stood to her feet. "You can have a seat," she said, pointing to a tan couch and matching chairs in the waiting area to the left of her desk. "Can I get you a cup of coffee or tea?"

"No thank you, ma'am. I'm fine."

The woman sat back down and continued typing.

"By the way, thank you for your help."

She smiled and answered an incoming call. "Martin, Hertz, and Prescott, how may I help you?"

Anna sat down on the firm, sleek sofa. She pulled a *Newsweek* from a stack of magazines fanned out on the glass coffee table but shoved the periodical back in its place. She didn't want to be perusing an article the first time she met her father.

Her father. The man until now she thought was dead. The man who gave her life.

Her mind raced with ways to introduce herself. *A handshake? Too formal. A hug? No. Way too informal... even though that would be wonderful. A handshake, definitely a handshake.*

Her stomach felt like she was on a roller coaster. Her palms were a puddle of sweat. She quickly searched her purse for a tissue to dab away the perspiration.

"Anna?"

She looked up and there he was, Andrew Prescott. He was just as she pictured. An attractive man in his early fifties with a slender build. His hair was grayer than she'd imagined, but the color made him look even more distinguished. Then she noticed his left eye slanted down a tad more than the right eye, just like hers. She smiled at the discovery.

People said she was the spitting image of Lydia. True, she had dark hair, a button nose, and small body frame. But she had her father's eyes.

Anna stood up and extended her arm. "Hello."

He glared at her gesture and stuck his hands in his pockets. "Diane, hold all my calls."

"Yes, Mr. Prescott."

Anna's smile faded.

Maybe he was nervous? After all, he'd started his day not knowing he would meet his daughter for the first time. Perhaps he wasn't one for public display of affection. It was only fair he'd get the benefit of the doubt.

She followed Andrew down the hallway to his office. He opened the heavy, wooden door and gestured for her to step inside when she let out an audible gasp. A mammoth, cherry desk was placed perfectly next to a window with a breathtaking view overlooking the Windy City and Lake Michigan. A glass-top conference table and six high-back chairs were on the other side of the room.

Photographs on display told the story of his lavish life. Several pictures depicted his love for boating. A professional portrait of what she assumed were his children—a boy and a girl—her half-siblings. And a picture of him dressed in a tuxedo kissing a beautiful blonde wearing a sparkling, champagne-tinted evening gown. Plaques and awards decorated his walls accompanied by bold paintings from contemporary artists. He had good taste, very good taste.

Anna was trying to absorb as much as possible about her father's life when the door slammed shut. Andrew sat behind his desk and leaned back in his chair. "What took you so long to find me?"

Not exactly the way she envisioned their first conversation, but they had to start somewhere. She sat down in the chair in front of his desk. "Actually, I just found out about you."

He frowned in disbelief. "What?"

"I was told my father died in a car accident before I was born."

He chuckled. "So, she killed me off, did she? Does Lydia know you're here?"

"No, she doesn't."

"Why not?"

Holding back tears, Anna replied, "She died...two weeks ago."

He blew out an exaggerated sigh. "Oh, I see. Now you want me to fill in the parental gap?"

"No. I...I just wanna get to know you. You're my father."

"Look, I'm sure you're a nice kid." He stopped, putting his hands up. "I mean young lady. But I have a wife and kids–"

"You mean my brother and sister," she said, pointing to the family picture.

He rose from his chair with his hands placed firmly on the desk. Leaning forward, he stared at her like she was his enemy. "Listen, I worked my butt off to get to where I am today. I have a good name in this city, and I won't have it dragged through the mud because one night I jumped in the sack with some hick."

He pulled out a checkbook from a drawer and slammed it shut.

"She was right," Anna whispered, "about...everything."

"Who?" he said.

"Momma. She said you weren't the person she thought you were...that you were cold and distant. But I didn't believe her. I wouldn't believe her. I thought if ya got a chance to meet me you'd–"

"What?" he asked with a cocky grin. "Bring you to my house for dinner? Look at my wife and say, 'Oh, by the way, honey, this is my daughter, Anna. I knocked-up her mom twenty years ago.' Then after we eat, we could clean out the spare room and turn it into your new bedroom. Is that what you thought? Just welcome you into the family and live happily ever after?" He snorted, filling out the check. "Like that would ever happen."

His cruel words and assailing tone shocked Anna. How could he be so indignant? How could her mother fall for a man so heartless and volatile? Then she realized what Lydia must have felt like the night Anna lashed out at her. She'd accused her of being selfish and hiding the truth to protect her image, but that wasn't true. She'd hid the truth to protect her daughter from this very moment.

"Ten thousand ought to do it."

"What?"

"Ten thousand dollars." His tone was so casual, as if the large amount of money was mere pocket change.

Anna felt her throat start to close. "Are you trying to pay me off?"

"Don't play dumb little country girl with me." He waved the checkbook in the air. "This is why you're really here."

"I don't want your money. I wanna be your daughter!" Tears raced down her cheeks. She covered her face with her hands, sobbing uncontrollably. Her body shook as she tried catching her breath.

"Fine," he barked, scribbling in a different amount. He tore the check from the book and held it out, waiting for her to take it. "There. Twenty thousand dollars. Not a penny more."

Anna's dream of having a father was over. She wiped away the tears with the back of her hand. "Ya never loved her, did you?" she said, sniffling. "She was just a naive girl you had some fun with to pass the time in a little hick town." She stared at the check. "And ya don't care about me, either."

He put the slip of paper in her hand. "Take it and leave."

He must have had a separate bank account because only his name appeared in the upper left corner of the check followed by a P.O. box number.

Anna walked toward the door. She turned around. "Perhaps paying people off is how you've kept such a good name in this city."

The corner of his lip snarled upward. If she were a man, he probably would have leapt over the desk and punched her.

"Don't worry, your dirty little secret is safe with me."

She held up the check and slowly ripped it into confetti, letting the tiny pieces fall to the floor. "Goodbye, Mr. Prescott."

Chapter Thirty Three

"That was the first and last time I saw him."

Anna wiped away the tears in her eyes before they had a chance to fall. She hadn't spoken to anyone about that day in Andrew's office expect Claire and Denny. Eight years was a long time, but not long enough for her to forget about the disastrous visit or, at the very least, be numb to it.

Confiding in Jake was cathartic. He was a good listener, better than she expected for a teenager. No interruptions. No questions. He quietly listened to how one incident had snowballed, redirecting the course of her life.

She told him about all the media jobs she'd applied for and that Channel 3 News made the first offer. The position hadn't mattered as much as the fact it was five hundred miles away from a life she wanted to forget. The job related to her journalism degree and that was good enough. She didn't even care which state she moved to. The farther away from Indiana, the better.

"Momma was my family, but she was gone. There was no reason for me to stay. That's why it was so easy to leave."

Exposing closet skeletons gave Jake the courage to bear his soul. He looked at Anna, as serious as she'd ever seen him. "I thought one day I was going to have a family, too."

Quietly she sat, giving him the same respect he'd given her when she exposed her wounds.

He looked down, gazing aimlessly at the kitchen table. "You know about the last foster home I was at? My arrest...for assault?"

Anna nodded. "Stephanie mentioned it."

"The guy deserved it. And worse."

"She said you hit him because he asked you to take out the garbage."

Jake smirked. "You don't know what really happened, do you?"

"What do you mean?"

"I'd won an art contest at school, and Shelly made a really big deal out of it. She fixed my favorite meal— lasagna." He smiled with a faraway look in his eyes. "She was a good cook. She wanted it to be a special night, but Ted ruined it. He came home late. And drunk. He got drunk a lot. He threw the dinner in the trash and tore up the picture I drew."

Jake had to stop and take a breath. "It was a picture of my mom and dad."

Anna's heart ached for Jake. She imagined the look on his face when that animal destroyed his picture. How could anybody be so cruel to a kid? She almost didn't want to hear the rest. "Then what happened?"

"Shelly tried stopping him, but that really ticked him off and he hit her. I knew he smacked her around, but it was the first time I actually saw him do it."

Jake looked away, but Anna knew what came next. "That's why you hit him, right?"

He nodded. "I thought he was going to kill me. So I ran to my room and locked myself in. I couldn't stay there anymore. I had to run away. But he called the police and told them I was the one who started it."

"Didn't Shelly tell them the truth?"

Jake shook his head. "She was so scared, she backed him up. I tried telling the cops what really happened, but nobody believes the foster kid, you know?"

Jake stood up and left the kitchen.

"Where are you going?"

"I need to get something. I'll be right back."

Anna knew the past few years of Jake's life hadn't been easy. To lose both parents in a short amount of time was bad enough, but she'd had no idea what all the fifteen-year-old had endured. His situation was worse than she thought. Living in fear under the same roof with an alcoholic wife beater, then getting arrested for protecting Shelly. Hearing Jake's story made her empathize with him even more.

As she sat at the table waiting for him to return, she was ashamed of herself. She'd had something he only dreamt about—a loving family. Her mother, Claire, and Denny did nothing but love her. And what did she do? How did she repay that love? With anger, bitterness, and resentment, all because she didn't know the truth about her father.

She'd found out the hard way that men like Andrew Prescott didn't know the first thing about love nor cared enough to learn. She sacrificed the most important relationship in her life for someone who wanted nothing to do with her. She'd cast herself in the starring role as the victim, convincing herself how bad her life turned out. She couldn't have been more wrong.

Drowning in a sea of guilt and regret, Anna heard a zipper slide open. Jake reached inside his backpack and pulled out a stack of photographs.

"After Dad died, Mom couldn't talk about him without crying so she just stopped talking about him altogether. She put his stuff in a box and threw it to the curb. I grabbed what I could."

He handed Anna the stack of pictures, their edges curled, of David and Faye, and some with Jake.

David was an attractive man, even more so in his police uniform. Jake had a strong resemblance to his father. The next photo was an action shot of Jake wearing a blue party hat and leaning onto the table to blow out a giant candle shaped as the number two on a white frosted cake.

As she went through the pile, Jake sat down. "I didn't get to see my dad a lot like other kids. He was a cop and had a crazy work schedule. A lot of nights and overnight shifts. Weekends and holidays too. But I was the only kid in my class who got to ride around in a police car a few times. Without handcuffs, that is. He'd let me sit up front and play with the siren. I used to pretend I was his deputy."

"It must have been hard not seeing him all the time."

"Sort of," he nonchalantly replied. "But when he wasn't working, he always made sure he spent time with Mom and me."

"What did you like to do?"

"Lots of stuff."

"Like what?"

"Let's see," he said, thinking back. "Movie night was once a month. He'd get pizza for dinner and the three of us would camp out in front of the TV with some DVDs. I never made it past the first one, and he'd have to carry me to bed."

Anna smiled. "What else?"

"He was a big sports fan. We were always tossing around a football or playing catch or shooting hoops. Even Mom joined in from time to time."

Anna giggled, trying to picture Lydia playing catch.

"We went to the park a lot, even if it was cold outside. I loved the playground. I think Dad did too, because he always went down the slide."

Anna couldn't picture Andrew going down a slide no matter how hard she tried.

"Dad really liked the outdoors. It's kinda funny though."

"What's that?"

"We never went fishing."

"Fishing?"

"Yeah, I always wanted to go. I don't know why, but I did."

He looked at Anna with a tinge of embarrassment in his eyes. "Sounds lame, huh? A city kid wanting to fish."

"Not to me it doesn't."

He smiled in relief.

Another photo showed David, Faye, and Jake posing in front of the Christmas tree. Jake's mile-wide smile said the Matchbox Race Car set he clung to was the big gift that year. She turned the picture in his direction. "How old were you?"

He leaned over to take a closer look. "Hmmm...eight, I think. That was our last Christmas together."

Anna was sorry she asked, but it didn't seem to bother Jake. They looked at the rest of the photos together, stopping occasionally as he explained the pictures. He seemed to enjoy reminiscing about his parents and the time they'd spent as a family.

Once they got through the pile, Jake reached into his backpack and pulled out David's police badge. He stared at it, rubbing his thumb across its brass surface before handing it Anna.

Finally, it all made sense. She pointed to the pictures and the badge. "Is this why you went back for your backpack the night of the robbery?"

Tears welled up in his eyes. "It's all I have left of them, Anna."

On the brink of tears herself, Anna replied, "I would have done the same thing."

Chapter Thirty Four

The Jeep was in park with the engine running as Anna sat in the driver's seat mustering up the courage to pull into the cemetery. She didn't know how long she'd been stalling, but it must have been a while.

An elderly man taking a morning stroll walked around the back of the vehicle. He stopped and turned around. He kicked his normal pace into a powerwalk, swinging his arms back and forth until he approached the driver's side. He tapped his finger on the window.

In Buffalo, Anna would've thought twice before rolling down the window to greet a strange man. But she was in Garrison.

She pressed the power button to the driver's window.

"You all right, miss?" he asked.

The white-haired man reminded her of Henry.

"Yes, I'm fine." She gripped the steering wheel as if she was about to continue driving.

A comforting smile eased across his sweet face. "Just take your time," he said, patting her forearm. "It's never easy saying goodbye."

"You're right. It's not."

He tipped his baseball cap. "Have a nice day, miss."

"Thanks, you too."

Anna watched the stranger resume his walk down the desolate road. Once he was out of sight, she took a deep breath and put the Jeep in drive. The ten miles per hour speed limit felt fast on the bumpy dirt path.

She hadn't been to her mother's grave since the funeral, but she knew exactly where she was buried as if she visited her every day for the past eight years.

Coming around the corner, a pink, heart-shaped headstone near a two hundred-year-old oak tree stuck out among the trite, gray headstones. She parked off the shoulder of the path, grabbed the flowers lying on the front seat, and got out. Her purse was inside the Jeep. No one was around to take it. It was just her and a bunch of bodies.

Gripping the bouquet, Anna stepped onto the freshly mowed grass. Her mind argued with her heart to leave. It wasn't too late. No one had forced her to come or to stay. All she had to do was turn around and drive away.

But she didn't.

The closer to the grave she got, the more reasons she came up with not to be there, until she reached her mother's final resting place.

She slowly knelt, staring at the headstone. "Hi, Momma." Her voice refused to go above a whisper. She placed the flowers in front of the cement block. "I brought you your favorite. White roses."

Her finger skimmed the inscription as she read it aloud.

Beloved Mother and Friend
LYDIA ANN SUTTON
BORN JUNE 22, 1968 - DIED MAY 23, 2011

The words turned blurry. She sniffled. "I know it's been a long time. I'm sorry I haven't visited you."

Her eyes were squeezed shut but tears broke through. "I wish I could take back everything I said and everything that happened. But I can't."

Anna slumped forward, hands braced on her knees. "I'm sorry I didn't listen to you. You were right about everything." She swiped at her face, but the tears didn't stop. "I'm so sorry I said those horrible things to you. I'd do anything just to have you back for one day."

Saying sorry once wasn't enough. It would never be enough.

"I wish you were here, so I could tell you how much I still love you."

Kneeling on the ground, pouring her heart out, Anna felt a hand gently touch her shoulder.

"She knows."

She whipped her head around and looked up. "Pastor Gill?" She sniffed, drying her drenched face with her hands. "What are you doing here?"

"Mrs. Beaumont went home to be with the Lord."

Anna should've known he had a funeral. The black suit he had on gave it away.

"Oh, I'm sorry to hear that."

"Don't be."

His carefree response left her bewildered. She gawked at him waiting for an explanation.

"She was ninety years old. Enjoyed every bit of life. One morning, she ate breakfast, took a nap, and that was it. If ya ask me, that's the best way to go."

Anna wiped her hand under her nose. Her tone turned brash. "Yeah, well, not everyone is as lucky as Mrs. Beaumont."

Pastor Gill didn't need her to elaborate. He knew what she meant.

With a deep sigh, he squatted down and clasped his hands together. "I know it doesn't seem fair, what happened to Lydia."

"You got that right."

"If she were here and had to do it over again, she'd get in that car and wouldn't think twice about it."

Anna turned her head away from him. "Why are you telling me this?" she snapped.

"Anna, she loved you."

"I know that."

"But as much as she loved you, God loves you more." Pastor Gill put his hand on her shoulder. "No matter how hard you try to hate Him or act like He doesn't exist, He loves you. And He'll never stop."

She turned and looked at him. As if all the emotion she

had inside has suddenly been sucked out of her, she asked in a childlike manner, "Why did she have to die?"

Pastor Gill looked as if he was about to cry himself. His voice softened. "I don't know and I don't pretend to know either. There are things in life that can't be explained. And even if I did have an answer, it wouldn't make it any easier."

Anna's face tightened. Her mouth opened as her lips quivered. She poked her chest with her finger. "Me. She died because of me. It's my fault! I killed her!" The floodgate inside her broke open as she screamed out her admission and she bawled like a baby.

Pastor Gill cupped his hands around her face. "Anna, ya have to stop blaming yourself."

She looked up at him. Her voice turned hoarse. "It's too hard. I can't."

"Yes, you can, but only by letting God back in your life. He's been waiting for you. He's the only one who can take away that guilt you've been feeling and give you the peace you've been longing for."

He hugged her tight as she sobbed in his arms. It was the kind of hug she'd needed from Andrew but didn't get.

"Don't give up on God, Anna. He hasn't given up on you."

Chapter Thirty-Five

Anna's body was pressed against the wall. Her stare drove past rows of chairs and landed on two large pieces of wood forming a cross at the altar. It felt so far away from where she stood in the back of the sanctuary. She needed to get closer.

Her slow descent down the aisle forced her to go to the past. Faces of mourners flashed before her. The sounds of their sniffles echoed in her head. All three hundred seats had been filled the day of Lydia's funeral. When there was no place left to sit, people lined up against the walls. Groups of children sat on the floor in the last row.

Once Anna made it to the front row, she sat in the first seat—the same one she had at the funeral. Claire had sat next to her, holding her hand throughout the service while her other hand gripped a crumpled tissue to wipe her tears.

From the corner of her eye, she noticed a bulletin lying in the middle of the row. It must have been left behind from last week's service. She picked it up and glanced at the cover with a scripture written out at the bottom of the page.

For God so loved the world he gave his only Son that who believes in Him shall not perish but have everlasting life.

Everlasting life. Eternity. Heaven.

Clinging to the knowledge that Lydia was in Heaven was the only comfort that kept Anna from going off the deep end. Even though she'd severed her relationship with God, she still believed in His existence. She couldn't deny the reality of Heaven.

Staring at the bulletin in her hands and the scripture on the page brought her back to the time she spent in a small classroom down the hallway.

She was five years old when she understood what it meant to be a Christian. During a Sunday School class, the teacher talked about Jesus being the way to salvation and spending eternity in Heaven. She went around the room asking each child if they'd invited Jesus into their hearts. One by one, each student responded, "Yes."

"What about you, Anna?" the teacher asked. "Have you accepted Jesus into your heart?"

Looking down at the table, she shook her head. She knew there was a God, and she knew His son was Jesus. But on a warm September morning, she chose to make Him her Savior.

With her head bowed and eyes close, she felt seven pairs of eyes watch her repeat the teacher in a prayer of salvation. She acknowledged Jesus as the Son of God and promised to live for Him, to love Him, and to put Him first above everything and everyone.

That moment in the classroom was innocent and pure. It

seemed so easy to believe and trust in God. She never thought the day would come when everything she believed to be true would change and that she'd be angry enough with God to shut Him out of her life.

Now decades later, Anna was back in the same church seeking to restore a relationship she'd abandoned. But she was all alone. No one was there to lead her in a prayer. It was just her and God.

Anna walked to the altar, clutching the bulletin. She wrestled to form the perfect introduction to her prayer. Then she was reminded that God wasn't seeking perfection. He wasn't going to judge her on how articulate she was or wasn't. He was simply there waiting.

Gazing at the cross, she pondered the bittersweet sacrifice Jesus made for her and everyone else who chose to believe in Him. A tear ran down her cheek. Then another. And another. Her legs gave out and she fell to her knees weeping.

Andrew's rejection had shattered her dream of having a father. But as she sobbed at the foot of the altar, she realized her true father had been with her all along. The best father anyone could ever want or ask for.

Through her tears, she uttered, "Forgive me, Father."

Anna hated being late, but she made an exception as she

glanced at her watch to see it was ten minutes after ten.

A packed parking lot of cars surrounded her as the muffled sound of music seeped through the closed doors of Garrison Community Church.

She threw her purse over her shoulder and walked toward the building with her eyes fixed on the steel cross at the roof's peak. She took a deep breath and opened the glass double doors.

A smiling woman holding a stack of bulletins stood outside the sanctuary entrance tapping her foot. She handed Anna a flyer with a hearty, "Good morning," and gave her a hug.

The upbeat song didn't ring a bell. Maybe it was new. Maybe the worship band had been playing it for a while. Anna hadn't listened to Christian music in years. She didn't know what was popular.

Starting as a spectator, she watched the sea of hands lifted high in the air while the rest of the congregation members clapped on beat.

An older man in his sixties strolled up and down the end of the aisles, pointing and counting the number of people in each row. He was jotting down the numbers on a scrap of paper when he saw Anna. Immediately, he walked over to her. His shiny, metal name tag read, "Usher."

He put his arm around her shoulder and leaned into her ear, projecting his voice over the music. "Can I help you find a seat, miss?"

"No, thank you. I need to do something first," she replied.

He smiled and patted her shoulder. "Okay. If ya need me, just give me a wave." Then he continued with his head count.

Anna rose on her tippy toes and scanned the audience from side to side until she spotted who she was looking for.

A few whispers and pointing accompanied stares of shock as she passed each row. Taking attention away from God wasn't her intention, but she had to see Carl. She'd kept him waiting eight years. She couldn't let him wait another minute.

She tapped him on the shoulder. He turned around and instantly stopped clapping. His hands dropped to his side. Mavis stood next to him and leaned over enough to be seen.

But all Anna saw was the man who risked his life to save her mother. She wrapped her arms around his neck and hugged him tight. He must have been in shock because his arms didn't leave his sides.

"Thank you for trying to save her," she whispered in his ear.

The faint sound of sniffles somehow drowned out the music. He embraced her and wiped his hand across his tear-filled eyes. Anna kissed his cheek and spotted Claire two rows up across the aisle. She went to her longtime friend, hoping to make amends.

"Claire, what happened the other night..."

Claire folded her arms across her chest. Anna had never

seen her look so cold. "Yeah, what about it?"

"You were right about everything. I'm sorry. I hope you can forgive me."

Her stoic stare morphed into a smile. "Now, what do you think?" she quipped, letting out snort. She pulled Anna in close, hugging her as she swayed her back and forth in her arms. She pointed to the empty chair next to her. "I knew one day you'd be back."

"What made you so sure?"

"Oh, a lot of praying." She stopped. Her countenance turned serious. "And cuz your Momma raised you right."

On the way to her seat, Anna gave Denny a hug.

"There's my Anna Banana," he joked.

Jake and Melanie were in the row in front of her. She tapped him on the shoulder. He turned around and had a confused look on his face. "Why are you here?"

"Same reason you are."

He smiled. "Glad you could make it."

"Me too, Jake."

"Hi, Miss Sutton," Melanie said. "It's good to see you."

"Thanks, Melanie."

Anna made eye contact with Pastor Gill on the altar. From the pulpit, he flashed a smile.

It was good to be home.

Chapter Thirty-Six

A cloud of steam followed Jake out of the bathroom. Standing in the hallway drying his hair with a towel, he called out, "Anna, we're almost out of shampoo. Could you–"

He stopped rubbing his head when he didn't see her in the family room. Tossing the towel over his shoulder, he went to her bedroom.

Slowly pushing the door open, he peeked his head around the corner. "Anna? Are you in there?" His faced crinkled when he saw the empty room.

Jake continued using the semi-wet cloth to dry his hair as he went into the kitchen. The crease in his forehead formed a deep gap when he noticed a piece of paper on the table. He read it out loud:

Meet me at the diner at 6. Anna.

He glanced at the clock. It was five thirty.

He picked up the note and read it again, making sure he hadn't overlooked a clue or indication to shed some light on her unexpected disappearance. He shrugged his shoulders and finished drying his hair before changing into a pair of black shorts, white T-shirt, and sandals.

The half-mile walk from the cottage to the diner had gotten easier over the past two months.

Jake was in the parking lot when he stopped dead in his tracks. The lights inside were off, but the parking lot was filled with cars. The sign hanging on the door said "Open" but no one was inside. First a cryptic note, now this? Something was very wrong. As he cautiously approached the entrance his imagination took off, thanks to all the crime dramas and real-life murder mystery documentaries he'd seen on TV.

What if she was kidnapped and forced to write the note? What if he took her to the diner to rob it and used her as a hostage? What if there was a mass shooting and everyone's dead?

It was always small, quiet towns like Garrison that made national headlines. The peaceful, rural communities where everyone knew everyone and there wasn't a hint of malice. The kind of place where nothing out of the ordinary ever happened—until that one day.

Jake hesitated, thinking about what he might discover on the other side of the door. He wanted to go for help, but first he had to see what was waiting for him inside. He had to see what, or who, was in the diner.

Before the chrome bells stopped jingling when he opened the door, the lights flew on. Jake's mouth hung open as dozens of people hiding behind the counter jumped up and yelled, "Surprise!"

Colorful balloons and a banner that read "Happy 16th Birthday, Jake!" hung from the ceiling. Food platters filled with chips, pizza, large bowls of pasta and potato salads, and a tangy homemade beverage in a large punch bowl took up an entire table. Gifts were piled high on a second table nearby.

He stared at Anna in bewilderment. "How did you know it was my birthday?"

"Our good friend, Stephanie," she replied with a hint of sarcasm.

All the teens from youth group, along with Pastor Gill, Al Parker, and Carl and Mavis Jenkins, were there to celebrate Jake's first milestone birthday. Partygoers lined up one by one offering their congratulations. Melanie waited at the end of the line.

"Happy Birthday, Jake," she said, giving him a hug and kiss on the cheek.

He slipped his arm around her waist. "Thanks, Mel."

Every time he was with sweet Melanie, he lit up like a Christmas tree. The party was no exception. It was his day, but all he thought about was how beautiful she looked in her blue party dress and white, strappy high heels.

Claire could be seen behind the partition striking a match and quickly moving the lit stick up and down before blowing it out.

Denny held open the swinging kitchen door as she

appeared holding a giant cake with candles ablaze. She started singing happy birthday and everyone joined in.

Jake took Melanie's hand and led her up to the counter with him.

Claire carefully set down the cake and slid it toward him. "Well, go on now before we start a fire!"

In one blow, he extinguished all sixteen candles.

Anna was talking to Carl when she saw Melanie give Jake a kiss before going to the restroom.

Finally, he was alone.

"Excuse me, Carl. I'll be right back."

She went to the food table where Jake helped himself to a second piece of Claire's homemade chocolate cake. She tapped him on the shoulder. "Having fun?"

He turned around and smiled. "It's the best party I've ever had. Thanks, Anna."

"It was my pleasure." She glanced around the room. "You know, Jake, there's something I've been wondering."

"Yeah, what's that?" he asked, breaking off a piece of cake with his fork.

"Why didn't tell me about your birthday?"

He shrugged his shoulder, curling his upper lip. "I didn't want you to make a big deal about it." He stabbed the desert with his fork and popped it in his mouth.

She chuckled. "Too late for that, huh?"

He smiled and continued chewing.

"So, what's the real reason?"

He finished swallowing the piece of cake. "The truth?"

"Yeah, that would be nice."

"I thought you wouldn't care about me being alone on my birthday. But that's before I got to know you." He paused. "It's another reason I didn't want to come here."

Panning the room filled with decorations, friends, and enough cake to feed a small country, Jake gave a slow smile. "Guess I was wrong. Instead of being alone..."

Anna put her arm around his shoulder. "Instead, you're spending your sixteenth birthday with people who love you."

"Yeah." He popped another piece of cake in his mouth.

Standing next to Jake, Anna still found herself in awe of his transformation. She thought back to the night of the robbery. Something had told her, deep down, that he was a good kid. Funny how a few months took him from a bitter teenager destined for a hopeless life to a respectable young man with a future. She didn't take the credit. She knew it wasn't anything she'd done. His second chance came because he opened his heart to Jesus. He's the one who repaired years of damage, which reminded Anna the real reason she wanted to talk to Jake privately.

Searching through the mound of presents on the table, she found her gift underneath the pile in the back corner.

"I was going to give you this at the cottage, but I think now is a good time."

"Anna, the party is my present. You didn't have to get me anything."

"Oh. Well if you really don't want it, I guess–"

He called her bluff. "I didn't *say* I didn't want it."

They laughed.

"Here." She handed him the gift. "Happy Birthday."

He set his plate down on the food table and took the box wrapped in metallic blue and white paper. He gave it a little jiggle, pondering what could be inside. Quickly, he untied the thick, blue organza bow and tore off the wrapping paper like a kid on Christmas morning. He found a groove to the plain cardboard box, flipped up the lid, and removed a layer of white tissue paper. The smile on his face disappeared. Slowly, he lifted a photo album out of the box, staring at the cover with his father's police badge attached on the black leather book. The inscribed gold plate below it read, "The O'Connor Family."

"Denny mounted the badge and did the engraving."

Jake turned each album page filled with pictures from his past as if he was looking at them for the very first time.

She gently placed her hand on his shoulder. "Now you don't have to keep them hidden anymore."

His glossy eyes spoke volumes as he wrapped his arms around her. "This means more to me than you'll ever know." He squeezed her tighter. "Thank you."

"No, Jake, thank you."

He stepped back, wiping his eyes. "For what? I didn't do anything."

"Oh, yes you did. Turns out, you taught me a few things too."

Again, he embraced her.

Claire approached them holding a camera. "Hey, you two, picture time," she said, searching for the on/off button. "Denny got me this fancy new gizmo and I've been dying to try it out. Now let me see," she mumbled to herself. "Ah ha! Here it is!" She pressed the circular button.

Jake draped his arm around Anna's shoulder and proudly displayed his gift.

"Here we go. Ready...one, two, three."

Chapter Thirty Seven

Jake and Melanie swayed back and forth on the old porch swing.

"Don't you go and forget me," she said, trying to lighten the mood.

Jake stared at her soft hand in his. "That won't happen."

On the outside, her sweet smile stretched across the brave face she wore for him. Inside, her heart was breaking.

She wouldn't see him at the diner, at church, or at the cottage. She'd probably never see him again. But he'd always be a beautiful memory during the best summer of her life, one that would stay with her forever.

"I hope you'll write me, let me know how you're doing. I wouldn't mind if you called once in a while too."

Stroking her hand with his thumb, he nodded his head, agreeing to her requests.

Her mouth quivered as she held back crying because she knew if she did, she wouldn't stop. Her last moments with Jake were slipping away. She didn't want to spend them sobbing in his arms.

"I'll never forget you."

"Same here." His hand met her face, touching her cheek one last time. He leaned in and kissed her, wrapping his arms around her and whispered in her ear, "I love you."

A tear rolled down her cheek. "I love you too."

The endearing words were a sword piercing her heart. Five hundred miles kept their love apart. A long-distance relationship never came up. They both knew making that kind of commitment wasn't fair to either of them. Their summer romance began in Garrison and that's where it had to end.

From the end of the driveway, Anna cupped her hands around her mouth and called out, "Jake, it's time to go."

He sighed, loosening his grip. As he got to his feet, he held out his hand for Melanie to take a hold of. He kissed her forehead and wrapped his arm around her shoulder. She slipped her arm around his waist and they went down the squeaky wood planks to the end of the driveway.

Anna pushed the last suitcase into the trunk of the Jeep and shut the hatch.

Kicking a small section of gravel back and forth in the driveway, she stuck her hands into her pockets. "Well, I guess that's it."

Claire sighed. "Ya got everything?"

"Yeah, I think so."

"Maybe you should take another look inside, just to make sure. It'll only take a–"

"Claire." Denny slid his hand on his wife's shoulders, giving her a slight squeeze.

She took her husband's subtle cue. Patting his hand, she said, "I know, I know. It's time for her to go."

Denny pulled Jake in close for one of his famous bear hugs. "So long, son."

"Bye, Denny. Thanks again for helping Anna with my birthday gift."

"My pleasure."

Jake turned to face Claire. "Well, you're finally rid of me."

She blew a sigh through her pursed lips and waved her hand in front of her face. "You weren't so bad." She pulled out a folded white envelope from her back pocket and handed it to him.

"What's this?" he asked.

"Only one way to find out."

He squeezed the thick package. Lifting the unsealed flap, his jaw dropped when he saw the stack of cash inside. He thumbed through the twenty, ten, and one dollar bills. There was a couple hundred dollars in there. Maybe more.

"That's a little bonus I like to give all my hardworking employees."

"But Claire–"

Her hand shot up, halting him from saying another word. "It's yours."

He held up the money-stuffed envelope. "Why did you do this?"

"Cuz I *wanted to*," she said, putting her hands on her hips. "Remember, it's my diner. My rules."

He smiled. "Thanks."

"You're welcome. You take care now, ya hear."

"I will."

"Get good grades in school."

"Yes, ma'am."

"Stay outta trouble."

"Definitely."

"And don't forget about the folks in Garrison who love you."

Jake had finally found a place where he fit in. A place where he was accepted for being himself. A place where people didn't judge past mistakes but found the good in people. A place he would be proud to call home. And he had to leave.

Claire placed her hands on Jake's shoulders. "You're a fine young man. You keep your eyes on God, and He'll always take care of you."

He nodded and hugged her. "Bye."

"Bye, hon," she replied and kissed him on the cheek.

Watching their emotional goodbye brought tears to Anna's eyes. Without a word, she reached out and hugged Denny.

"My Anna Banana," he said, swaying her back and forth in his manly arms.

"Bye, Denny."

"Bye, sweetheart."

Anna looked at Claire. "You've done so much for me. Just saying thank you doesn't seem like enough."

Claire's dry, cracked hands cupped her face. "Seeing this smile again is all the thanks I need."

"I love you, Claire."

"I love you too, darlin'." She squeezed her tight with a hearty pat on her back.

Last time Anna left Garrison, she couldn't get out of town fast enough. Now, she didn't want to leave, but she had to get Jake back to the group home.

"All right, all right," Claire said, using her wrist to wipe away her tears. "You best be heading out if ya wanna make it home before dark."

"I'll call you when we get there."

"I'll be waiting."

Anna got in the Jeep as Jake gave Melanie one last hug goodbye. She turned the ignition and he pulled himself away from her. He got in the Jeep, shut the door, and sank into his seat, staring straight ahead.

She fastened her seatbelt and pointed to his buckle for him to do the same. She wanted to ask him if he was okay. She wanted to see if he wanted to talk. But she already knew what his answer would be. She put the Jeep in reverse and backed out of the driveway as Denny, Claire, and Melanie waved goodbye.

Anna and Jake spent the ride home to Buffalo the same

way they had on the way to Garrison. Only this time, his silence didn't bug her.

As long as the road trip was, she couldn't find anything to say either.

"There it is," Jake said, pointing to a large, two-story home. "The one with the pine tree."

It was the only time he'd spoken since leaving the cottage, except for the pit stop at a Subway in Sandusky when he ordered a large ham and turkey sub.

Easing up on the gas pedal, Anna put the blinker on and pulled into the short blacktop driveway where an audience of one waited to welcome them home.

The porch light shone down on Stephanie leaning against the doorway. Her stone-cold countenance made Anna feel like a teenager busted for breaking curfew.

She'd expected the cantankerous social worker to insist on picking up Jake at a neutral location. To her surprise, she'd allowed Anna to bring him home.

She put the Jeep in park while the engine ran and popped the trunk. "Do you need a hand with your stuff?"

"Na. I can get it," he said as he got out.

He pulled his suitcase from the top of the pile and tossed his backpack over his shoulder. He shut the hatch and came back around to the passenger side.

Stephanie had yet to go inside, making their goodbye awkward. Standing like a statue, she huffed and glanced at her watch.

Anna rolled down the window. "Well..." she said, tapping the steering wheel, searching for an articulate way to convey her feelings. "I guess this is it."

"Guess so," he replied, pulling up his backpack as it slipped down his shoulder.

"Goodbye."

"Bye, Anna."

She watched him walk up the driveway and thought to herself, *That's the best I could come up with? What's wrong with me?*

She leaned her head out the driver's side window. "Hey, Jake?"

He turned around.

She wanted to get out of the Jeep and hug him. She wanted to tell him if he ever needed anything to call her. She wanted to tell him she'll be praying for him. But she didn't say any of those things.

"Take care."

How lame. *Take care* was what you said to someone you didn't know. A person you were polite to, not someone you'd grown to love.

He smiled, echoing her sentiment. "You too."

She stayed in the driveway to see how his encounter with the social worker turned out.

"Hi, Stephanie. How's it going?" he asked.

Her rigid stance relaxed as she stammered, "H-hello, Jake. I'm well."

"Glad to hear it. Well, I gotta put my stuff away. See you later."

Her shocked disposition toward his pleasant demeanor was priceless. No doubt she expected the old Jake. The rude, disrespectful, disobedient orphan she came down hard on.

Her crossed arms dropped to her sides like hundred pound weights. She looked at Anna for an explanation.

Purposely looking clueless, Anna raised her eyebrows and shrugged her shoulders.

Stephanie spun around, went inside, slammed the door shut, and turned off the porch light.

Chapter Thirty Eight

Jake sat on the couch in the family room holding the TV remote, flicking listlessly through the stations. He circled back to the top of the channel list in a second attempt to find something to watch.

He'd been back at the group home for two days and was nothing short of a model citizen. He did his share of chores without complaining, kept his bedroom clean, and obeyed the rules.

But he preferred to be alone with his summer memories of Garrison. He missed Claire's sass and Denny's humor. He missed his friends from youth group and Pastor Gill's sermons on Sundays. Most of all, he missed Melanie. She was constantly on his mind. There was no one like her. He didn't want anyone else.

With another click of the remote, Jake landed on Channel 3. The noon newscast had started. His thumb, poised in midair, was about to hit the button when a mugshot with the word ARRESTED underneath it caught his eye. The two people in the picture looked just like Bryce and Jordan. Jake turned up the volume and inched closer to the edge of the couch.

The anchor began the report. "Buffalo police say a pair of

teens' summer-long crime spree is over. Seventeen-year-old Bryce Lindell and sixteen-year-old Jordan Summers are accused of a string of armed robberies that began in May."

Video rolled of the teens being escorted out of police cars with their hands cuffed from behind. Their heads hung as a cluster of reporters yelled out questions while photographers fired off a barrage of flashes.

Bryce's dirty jeans and scruffy, untrimmed facial hair made him look like he'd been pulled from a dumpster. Jordan didn't look any better. He had on a stained, thin white T-shirt and ripped jeans. His buzz cut had grown and stuck out from under a faded blue baseball cap on backwards.

The anchor continued the report. "Police say the teens held up convenience and liquor stores, pawn shops, and gas stations. Officials say the teens eluded police for months until an anonymous caller tipped them off about an abandoned house on the east side where they found the suspects with cash, weapons, marijuana, and cocaine."

The footage rolled again, this time in slow motion. If Jake had gotten away the night of the robbery, he'd be on the tape walking behind Bryce and Jordan into the Erie County Holding Center.

"Lindell and Summers face several counts of armed robbery, drug possession, and assault charges from a robbery at Allen's Corner Store where the store owner fought back."

253

Mr. Allen's bloody hand flashed through Jake's mind. His family must have been terrified when they heard about the robbery.

What if the bullet had hit Mr. Allen instead of the window? What if Bryce had killed an innocent man for a measly fifty dollars?

The store owner was only trying to make a living, just like Claire. *What if someone stuck a gun in her face?* Jake shook his head, trying to erase the image.

Claire wasn't that different from Mr. Allen. She owned a small business, just like him. She worked hard, just like he did. And she played by the rules, just like him.

Had it not been for Mr. Allen dropping the charges, Jake would be in lockdown at Wyatt Hall. He wouldn't have had a second chance. His future would have been hopeless. He owed Mr. Allen.

Jake turned off the television and went to his bedroom to get his backpack.

Chapter Thirty-Nine

Tucked in the bottom corner of the window, a white sign in red capital letters read **HELP WANTED**.

Outside of Allen's Corner Store, Jake stared at the window where a bullet had been lodged three months ago. The cracked glass was gone, but the robbery was very much alive in his mind. The image of Bryce pulling the handgun out of his jacket pocket and sticking the weapon in Mr. Allen's face was more vivid now than when it happened.

He started having second thoughts about going inside. Turning around, he looked at Mandy, one of the aides from the group home who waited in her car across the street. She smiled and waved.

Butterflies fluttered feverishly in his stomach at the thought of seeing Mr. Allen. But Jake knew the time had come to make amends.

God, I need you. Please help me do this.

He took a deep breath and went inside.

Scratch-off lotto tickets filled a display case on the counter that blocked his view of Mr. Allen at the register. He watched the owner scan grocery items before announcing the total. "That'll be $19.24."

The customer handed him a twenty-dollar bill from her

wallet, then accepted her change and receipt.

Jake stepped casually toward the magazines and pulled a *Sports Illustrated* from the rack. Holding it up high enough to cover part of his face, he glanced over the top watching the store owner bag the woman's groceries.

"You're all set, Gretchen." Mr. Allen smiled and slid the bag to her. "Tell Roger I hope he feels better soon. And if you need any help around the house, just give me a call."

"Thanks, Mr. Allen. I'll let him know."

"Have a nice day."

She hoisted the bulky bag. "You too."

Jake was surprised at the friendly interaction. He'd never acted that way around Jake, Bryce, and Jordan. Then again, they'd never given Mr. Allen a reason to be nice. They were rude. They disrespected him. They loitered. They stole from him and held him at gunpoint. The man had every reason to have a chip on his shoulder.

Jake put the magazine back when he saw the woman struggling to get a good grip on the bag. He rushed to the exit and held the door open.

She was taken back by his polite gesture. "Why, thank you, young man."

He replied, "No problem."

She stepped outside, and he let go of the door as it swung shut. The store was empty. It was time.

Mr. Allen was meticulously lining up small cartons filled with Hershey bars on the shelves behind the counter when

Jake approached. His mouth went dry and his tongue felt like sandpaper.

"Excuse me. Mr. Allen?"

"Yeah," he said, looking up. In an instant, he recognized Jake and his skin turned flushed red. "Hey! You're that kid!"

"Yes, sir."

Reaching for the phone he shouted, "I'm calling the cops!"

"Mr. Allen, please put down the phone. I'm not here to cause trouble."

The store owner stopped dialing and turned around.

"I just want to talk to you for a second."

With a hearty huff, Mr. Allen slammed the phone on the hook. His hands slapped down on the counter as he leaned over. "What do you want?"

Jake reached into his backpack and pulled out the money Claire gave him. He squeezed the package. That kind of money to a teen was like winning the lottery. He could have done a lot with that cash. Get a new bike. Some cool video games. Better clothes. Or something much more noble.

He held out the envelope. "This is for you."

Mr. Allen's eyebrows squished together. Rows of wrinkles spread across his forehead.

"I want you to have it."

Cautiously, he reached for the envelope. He lifted the flap and saw the green stash. "You're giving this to me?"

"Yes, sir."

"Why?"

"Because it's the right thing to do."

Mr. Allen's expression softened.

"I know it's not enough to cover the broken window, but I'm going to get a part-time job after school and pay you back the rest. No matter how long it takes."

The red in the store owner's face began to fade.

"I'm really sorry about what happened. I hope one day you can forgive me."

Jake walked to the door and was almost out of the store when he heard, "Hey, kid."

He turned around.

Mr. Allen tapped the envelope in his hand. He jerked his head toward the window. "Grab me that sign."

Jake pointed to the help wanted sign.

"Yeah, that one."

He pulled it out and handed it to him.

Mr. Allen sighed. "Job is yours if you want it."

Jake's eyes grew wide. "Really? You're giving me the job?"

"Yeah, really. But I'm keeping my eye on you." He pointed and wagged his beefy finger in the teen's face. "Mess up once and you're outta here. Got it?"

Jake smiled. "Got it."

Two words Anna had been waiting a long time to type finally made it onto the page. *The End.* Her book was done.

She sent the cursor up to the cover page and marveled at the title: *Millionaire Murderer* by Anna M. Sutton.

Then she waited.

The thrill she'd expected to feel wasn't there. All that work, all that time, for what? Writing a novel was no small feat, but it didn't bring satisfaction like she'd assumed it would.

Her priorities had shifted. The proof was next to her.

She picked up a picture frame with the photograph of her and Jake from his party. His smile as he held the album made her smile. That's when she realized what was missing. She knew what she had to do.

Chapter Forty

"Excuse me," Anna said, tapping the window. "I have a ten o'clock meeting with Stephanie Grey."

The heavyset receptionist didn't flinch except for her eyes that darted up from the computer screen. She slid the glass open. "Your name?"

"Anna Sutton."

Pushing aside her frizzy bangs, she picked up the phone receiver and entered a three-digit extension on the keypad.

"Anna Sutton is here," she said and hung up. "She'll be out in a minute." Turning her attention back to the computer she mumbled, "Have a seat."

Anna sat down on a hard chair with a wobbly wooden arm. Noticeable cracks in the cream-colored walls and the gray concrete floor took her back to the night of Jake's arrest.

She searched for a magazine or newspaper. Unfortunately, there wasn't a thing to read to pass the time. All she had to look at were posters of smiling kids and adults advocating foster care and adoption. The cheery advertisements hung randomly in the dingy waiting room and failed to divert her attention from the depressing atmosphere the agency exuded.

Ten minutes passed before a door swung open and Stephanie appeared, perusing the contents inside a manila folder. "Come on back," she said. She avoided eye contact and continued reading the file as Anna followed her down to her office.

She stepped inside and sat on the metal folding chair she assumed was for her. There were no pictures or trinkets on Stephanie's desk. No colorful wall hangings to admire, not even a scrawny potted plant on the ledge of the glass block window. Just a small desk and two metal filing cabinets. Anna didn't know which was colder, the chair or the bleak office.

Stephanie closed the file and tossed it on a pile of folders. "What can I do for you?"

"How's Jake doing?"

She sat down in a battered chair. "No complaints. So far."

Still cynical. "That's good to hear."

The social worker leaned back. A loud squeak echoed in the room. "Come on, Anna, that's not why you came down here, now is it?" Her hands clasped together at her midsection.

"No, it isn't." she replied.

"Well, why did you? What's going on?"

Anna took a deep breath then blurted out, "I want to adopt Jake."

Darting upright in her chair, Stephanie let out a snort. "You're kidding."

"No, I'm not. I want to adopt Jake."

She stared at Anna like she had three heads. Funny the things a person can say to make someone speechless.

"I want to be his mom. I want us to be a family."

"Anna, you don't have to do this."

"I know I don't *have* to do this. I *want* to do this. There's a difference."

"Adoption isn't like going to a clothing store and picking out a shirt you like."

What a lame analogy. Couldn't she have come up with something more creative than that?

"There's a lot to consider."

"Like what? Enlighten me."

"The waiting list, for starters. It's a mile long for couples who want to adopt."

"Infants," Anna interjected. "Couples who want infants are waiting a long time. I'm sure it's a different story for older kids. Really, Stephanie, how many parents do you think are looking to adopt a sixteen-year-old?"

She squinted her beady eyes. "Okay, how about the fact that the courts favor married couples? You didn't by any chance get hitched in the last two months, did you?"

"That sounds like discrimination to me."

She sighed and came back swinging in the third round, saving the best for last. "How do you intend to support Jake?" Her voice was calm. She folded her hands together with a smug look on her face. "If I'm not mistaken, your current employment status is unemployed."

Stephanie hit Anna where it really hurt—her pride. Speaking to her as if she was incapable of holding down a job made her want to reach across the scuffed desk and smack that smirk right off her face. But something stopped her, gently reminding her who was really in charge. Suddenly, she felt peace in the midst of a storm. She recognized the Holy Spirit nudging her. God had set a plan in motion long before becoming a mom ever became a notion. If He wanted her to take care of Jake—and she was certain He did—no opposition, no matter how strong, would prevent His plan from being carried out. It felt good having someone else fight for her. It was nice to know she wasn't alone. God was with her.

Anna crossed her legs and sat back in the uncomfortable chair. "You're right, Stephanie. I don't have a job—at the moment. But you and I both know that is my choosing."

The social worker's cocky grin slowly dissipated.

"We both know I'm an educated woman with work experience. I can get a job, a good job, like that," she said, snapping her fingers. "So money really isn't an issue either. Is it?"

Anna thought she won the war. She'd debunked every notion Stephanie hurled her way. But it wasn't enough.

"I admit Jake has changed," Stephanie said, relaxing her posture. "But adoption is a major, life-changing commitment, not a few months in the sticks. Get my drift?"

"Yeah, I get it. Social status and money are more important than what's best for Jake. What I don't get is–"

"Look–"

Anna's hand shot straight up. "I'm not finished," she said as politely as she could.

Stephanie sighed and folded her arms across her chest. "Go on."

"Thank you. As I was saying, what I don't get is why you're making this so difficult. I thought you'd be thrilled that Jake has a chance at a real family."

"Anna, parenting is a big responsibility. I just feel you may regret your decision. Right now, Jake is doing fine. But what if this new behavior doesn't last? He could pick up where he left off and then what would you do? What if you get a phone call in the middle of the night from the police, like I did? What would you do? Take him back to Garrison for a few months for another round of rehab?"

"You don't have any faith in him at all, do you?"

"You've known him for a few months. I've known him for years."

"Yeah and look how he turned out after two months with me."

Stephanie's nostrils flared. "I know what he is capable of. He needs someone to keep him in line, someone with a tight rein on him so he doesn't go back to that group of thugs."

Keep him in line? A tight rein? Finally, it clicked.

"That someone you're talking about is you?"

"I didn't say that."

"You didn't have to."

Stephanie fidgeted in her chair, letting out an exasperating sigh.

"This isn't about Jake. This is about you, Stephanie, and your need for control. Because that's when you feel powerful. When people like that kid have no say in the matter."

The social worker flung her arms in the air. "Let's not go down that road again!"

"You're right, let's not. Let's take a different road." Anna leaned forward, resting her fists on the desk. "How about the road where you actually help Jake by helping me get custody?" She pointed at her with authority. "Because deep down, you know it's the right thing to do."

Stephanie sat silently with a glare hotter than a laser beam.

"I don't care how long it takes. I don't care how many papers I need to fill out or how many times I have to go to court. My mind is made up. I'm adopting Jake." Anna slung her purse over her shoulder and marched to the door. Before leaving, she spun around. "You better get the ball rolling. You have a lot of work to do."

Chapter Forty One

Anna stared out the café window watching the orange and yellow leaves on a maple tree fall to the ground. The shining sun made up for the breezy October afternoon. The bistro table on the patio was the perfect place to finish her cup of green tea.

She snugged her cardigan sweater around her and grabbed her purse. She was about to get up when Henry arrived.

"Hi, Anna. Sorry I'm late."

She stood up and gave him a hug. "Thanks for coming."

They went inside and sat down in a corner booth.

"You spiked my curiosity when you said it was important."

By the time he removed his jacket, the waitress approached them holding a tablet and pen, ready to take their order.

"Hi folks, what can I get for you today?"

Henry opened the menu, scanning the limited lunch choices. "I'll have the ham and swiss cheese sandwich on rye, mustard, no onions, and a black coffee."

"Sure thing. And you, miss?"

"The grilled chicken salad with honey mustard dressing,

and can I get refill of green tea, please?"

"You got it." The waitress stuffed the notebook in her apron pouch, scooped up the menus, and went to the kitchen to put the orders in.

"I take it your trip to Garrison went well," Henry said.

Anna tilted up her chin. "What makes you think that?"

He shrugged his shoulders. "Would you have wanted to see me if it hadn't?"

"Probably not. Although it would've been fun to see the look on your face when you found out you were wrong."

They both chuckled.

"Actually, my summer with Jake turned out better than I expected. For both us."

While waiting for their food, Anna filled Henry in on all that happened from Jake's job at the diner, to Melanie, and most importantly, his new-found faith in Jesus.

"Church? Wow, didn't see that one coming."

"Me either. Funny thing is, he fits right in...like he was meant to be there. But then again, aren't we all?"

He smiled weakly, as if he didn't know how else to respond.

Anna had talked to Henry about all kinds of topics—politics, current events, sports, and the environment. But God was never one of them. She wasn't sure where he landed on the subject. She hoped that one day he'd make the same decision Jake had.

The waitress returned carrying two plates. Henry

munched on his sandwich, listening intently to Anna lead up to her adoption plan. In between bites of her salad, she recapped the unpleasant details of her not-so-encouraging meeting with Stephanie.

His countenance morphed to distress in a matter of minutes. He picked up his mug. "I hate to say it, Anna, but she may be right."

"Wait a minute. Are you siding with the opposition?"

He smiled through the concern on his face. "Adoption isn't as easy as you think." He drank the last swig of coffee.

"I never said it was going to be easy. Nothing in life worth fighting for is. But I'm going to adopt Jake."

The waitress came back over to their booth. "Can I get you anything else?"

Anna looked at Henry and he shook his head no.

"Just the check, please," Anna said.

She ripped off the order from her notepad and placed it face down in the middle of the table. "There you go."

"Thanks." Anna reached across the avocado-colored table and slid the bill toward her.

Henry took the slip out of her hands. "No, no, no. I got it."

"I invited you, remember?"

"Yes, I know," he said, pulling his wallet from the back pocket of his pants. "But I insist." He smiled and tossed enough cash to cover the bill and the tip next to the salt and pepper shakers.

Anna downed the remaining tea. "Look, Stephanie is

going to do whatever she can to make me throw in the towel on this adoption. But she's got another thing coming. I don't give up that easily."

"Ahh, there it is...that fire. Nice to see you've still got it."

"You bet I do. I'm not going to sit back and leave Jake's fate in the hands of a disgruntled social worker. That's why I need a plan, starting with people who will vouch for my character. You're at the top of my list. Who better to have in my corner than one of the city's most respected judges?" She gave an exaggerated wink.

"Flattery will get you nowhere, Anna."

They chuckled.

"Listen, you know you can count on me. But–"

"Henry, Jake belongs with me. It's that simple."

"I know that, and you know that." He shoved his wallet back in his pocket. "But convincing a judge, to be honest–"

"You always are."

He sighed. "Anna, some things in life are...impossible."

Three months ago, the word *impossible* was like a brick fortress in front of her. No way around it. No way over it.

Not anymore.

She stared into the judge's handsome blue eyes, leaned across the table, and placed her hand on top of his. "Henry, with God all things are possible."

He squeezed her hand. "I hope you're right."

She picked up her purse, slid across the faux leather seat, and left the café with him.

"Thanks again for lunch. Next time, it's on me," she said.

He smiled. "Okay, I'll hold you to that." He leaned over and hugged her goodbye. "Whatever you need, Anna, I'm here for you."

She kissed him on the cheek. "Thanks, you're a good man."

He winked and waved. "See you later."

"Bye, Henry. See you in court."

Chapter Forty-Two

Jake had been given a second chance at life. An opportunity to make right all that had been wrong. School was no exception. He started his junior year on a mission to bring his disappointing D average to a respectful B, and hopeful for an A by the end of the year.

The first quarter proved to be challenging. He was tempted to give up more than once. But the thought of wearing a blue cap and gown, walking across the stage, and being handed his diploma pushed him to keep going.

Tutoring sessions with teachers caught him up to speed with the rest of his classmates. He even managed to fit in an after school activity when the new art teacher, Mrs. Randolph, noticed his drawing talent and encouraged him to join the art club.

Juggling a full course load at school and his part-time job at Allen's Corner Store, Jake didn't have time to get into trouble even if he wanted to.

Twice a week, he worked a four-hour shift after school. After punching out at seven o'clock, it was back to the group home where he snagged a sandwich or leftovers for a late dinner and stayed up until ten o'clock doing homework.

Jake's job was far from glamorous, but he liked working

for Mr. Allen who kept him busy stocking shelves, mopping the floor, and waiting on customers.

"Your total comes to $18.56."

The young man in his early twenties reached into the front pocket of his jeans, pulled out a twenty-dollar bill, and handed it to Jake. The black sweatshirt with orange lettering and matching baseball cap both read "Buffalo State," a good indication the customer was a student at the nearby college.

Jake punched in the dollar amount and the register drawer popped out. "A dollar forty-four," he said, handing the customer his change and receipt. He slid the double-bagged groceries across the counter. "Have a nice day."

"Thanks, you too."

Jake finished replenishing the candy aisle with Kit Kats, Milky Ways, and M&Ms when Mr. Allen walked into the store carrying a pizza. The aroma seeping from the cardboard box made Jake's stomach rumble in hunger.

The store owner lifted the box in the air announcing, "Dinner."

Saturday was Jake's longest shift, and Mr. Allen always ordered food for them to share.

In between waiting on customers, they chowed down on take-out and had become very social with each other. Jake discovered Mr. Allen had quite a sense of humor. His hearty chuckle at his own corny jokes made Jake laugh more than the punch lines.

Between Claire's bonus and his paycheck from the store, Jake paid off the damage to the window in two months. But even after that, he kept working at the store, looking forward to the unexpected camaraderie he and the storekeeper had developed.

Chapter Forty Three

A faint voice coming from the other side of the door called out, "Who is it?"

Anna leaned toward the door. "Mrs. Elardo, it's me." She raised her voice a notch. "Anna Sutton."

Immediately, she heard a bunch of locks unlocking. The door opened and her landlord stood there, wearing her signature floral housecoat and pink, fuzzy slippers.

"I hope you don't mind me dropping in like this. I had a craving for cake." Anna held up a square box. "I was wondering if you wanted to join me."

The old woman's eyes grew wide as she gasped. "I'd love to, dear! Come in, come in." She latched her cold, boney fingers onto Anna's forearm and drew her inside.

"It's store bought. I'm not much of a baker."

"Oh, that's fine, dear. I'm sure it's delicious." She shut the door and relocked all the locks.

It was the first time Anna had been in the landlord's apartment. Illumination from the television and a dim desk lamp gave off the only light in the tiny living room. An episode of *Family Feud* with Richard Dawson was on. The host had his arm around a pretty blonde contestant with feathered hair that resembled Farrah Fawcett's famous do.

Mrs. Elardo shuffled to a faded brown tweed recliner and picked up the remote to turn off the set. "Let's go in the kitchen," she said, leading the way. "We'll be more comfortable in there."

She turned on the light, and Anna set the dessert on a small square wooden table.

A whiff of baked sugar escaped as she lifted the front flap. Carefully, Anna removed the three-layer cake from the box.

"Oh, it's chocolate. Chocolate is my favorite!" Mrs. Elardo clasped her hands together. "But I guess all old ladies love chocolate."

Anna smiled. "It's my favorite too."

"Would you like some coffee or tea?"

"Tea, please."

She went to the counter and took off the lid to a beige canister. Bringing the ceramic container closer to her face, she squinted. Her smile dropped.

"Something wrong?"

She clutched the canister in grief. "I'm sorry, dear. All I have is green tea."

The irony amused Anna. "Green tea is fine with me, Mrs. Elardo."

"Oh, good," the old woman said with a sigh of relief. "Two green teas coming up!" She filled a small teapot with water and put it on the stove.

"Would you like me to get some plates and forks?"

"Oh, yes, dear. Thank you. The plates are up in that cabinet and the forks are over there," she said, pointing to the first drawer below the cupboard. Mrs. Elardo waited at the stove for the water to reach a roaring boil.

Anna opened the cupboard doors and was troubled by what she saw. Three plates, three drinking glasses, and two mismatched mugs took up a small section of space on the bottom shelf. She peered into the stainless steel sink. Not a plate or glass in need of washing. And she didn't have a dishwasher. She opened the utensil drawer, not surprised to find a few forks, spoons, and knives.

Seeing the minuscule kitchenware collection made Anna realize how alone Mrs. Elardo really was. She felt her landlord's heartache for companionship as if it were her own. Anna didn't like it, not one bit.

The whistle from the teapot shrieked. Anna took two plates, forks, mugs, and a cutting knife for the cake to the kitchen table where Mrs. Elardo waited with the teapot and tea bags.

She prepared each mug as Anna sliced into the decadent dessert, carefully removing a large piece. The dense hunk of cake tipped over on its side.

"Thank you, dear." Mrs. Elardo smiled broadly as she took the dessert plate.

"You're welcome."

Anna cut a smaller piece for herself. She was still working on shedding those last couple of pounds that had made their way to her hips thanks to Claire's home-cooked meals.

Mrs. Elardo dug into her piece of cake. Her eyes danced with joy the instant the chocolate dessert hit her taste buds. She let the fork linger in her mouth as her thin lips worked hard to scrape off every ounce of creamy frosting stuck to the utensil. Then she chewed as if in slow motion, enjoying every morsel.

Anna had known Mrs. Elardo for eight years, but she couldn't recall a time when she'd seen her so happy. She was amazed at how something as simple as a piece of cake and company could brighten a person's mood.

In between bites, they made small talk. Mrs. Elardo's had finished half of her piece when she asked out of the blue, "Why did you really come here, dear?"

Anna wiped her mouth with a napkin. "The truth?"

She nodded.

"I know it's hard living by yourself. When you're alone, there's no one to talk to or spend time with. Sometimes it's nice to have someone to go shopping with or go for a walk in the park with. Those little things that a lot of us take for granted. And, well…"

Mrs. Elardo leaned across the table. "And what, dear?"

Anna nervously played with her fork, tapping the base as it teetered on the edge of the plate. She chose her words carefully. She didn't want to offend her. But honesty prodded her heart.

"Well, I felt God wanted me to visit you."

Anna expected confusion but Mrs. Elardo listened intently, waiting to hear more.

"I thought about you by yourself, no one to talk to or laugh with, and thought you could use some company."

Tears filled her eyes and her bottom lipped quivered.

Anna patted the older woman's hand. "You're a sweet lady, Mrs. Elardo, and I just want to let you know God loves you."

She reached into the front pocket of her housecoat, pulled out a hanky, and dabbed her wet eyes. Then she picked up her mug and raised it high. "Salute."

Anna lifted her mug. "Salute." They softly clanked the cups together and drank the tea.

They spent the next two hours talking. Anna learned Mrs. Elardo was more than an elderly woman who lived on the second floor and collected the rent.

A sparkle twinkled in her eye as she relived her past, starting with her humble upbringing as one of three girls in a tiny apartment in North Buffalo. But her face lit up when she went back in time to the night when she met her husband at a dance hall during the Korean War.

Anna could hear the saxophone wailing as Mrs. Elardo described the room packed with couples twirling to the beat of the swing music. She had just sat down at a table when her eyes met his. It was truly love at first sight. Their brief courtship lasted a week. The young solider received his orders to leave for battle and the day before he left, they got married at city hall—just the two of them. Her only contact with him for two years had been through the letters that Mrs. Elardo still had. She even pulled out a few and read them out loud for Anna.

Anna bent down and hugged Mrs. Elardo.

The embrace seemed to catch her off guard, but she quickly reciprocated the gesture. Anna was halfway out the door when she made a bold move.

"Anna?"

She turned around.

A nervous gaze fell across her face. "Would you like to come over tomorrow night and help me finish the cake?" She held her breath, gripping her hands as she waited for a reply.

Anna smiled. "I'd love to, Mrs. Elardo."

She sighed. "Same time?"

"I'll be here."

"Oh, good." Her smile stretched from one side of her face to another.

"I'm sure you have more stories to tell."

"Do I!" she exclaimed, throwing her arms in the air.

"Can't wait to hear them. See you tomorrow."

"Good night, dear."

Chapter Forty Four

Anna returned to her apartment, locked the door, and dropped her keys into her purse that sat on a three-tiered stand near the doorway.

She took the TV remote off the coffee table, hoping a mindless show would make her tired enough to sleep. A corny sitcom, an outlandish reality show, a bizarre syndicated talk show, anything that didn't require thinking.

After channel surfing and coming up short, she turned off the set and flung the remote to the opposite end of the couch. A wave of loneliness rushed over her as she looked around her empty apartment.

Being alone had never bothered her before. She chose a life of seclusion after her mother died and treasured her privacy.

But things changed.

She went to the kitchen, flicked on the light, and pulled the tea canister toward her. She removed the lid and reached inside. Her fingertips hit the bottom and jumped from side to side hunting for a tea bag. Nothing.

Her shoulders sank. "Great," she huffed, forcing the lid back onto the canister.

Peering at the hanging clock, the night was closing in on

eleven. Mr. Allen's store was still open. She could be there and back in fifteen minutes.

Anna grabbed her purse, digging through the cluttered bag when a déjà vu moment struck her. The night of the robbery. She'd gone to the store for tea.

The holdup happened so fast, but every detail remained crystal clear in her mind. The loaded gun. Jake's panic-stricken face. Mr. Allen's fight and injury.

The metal keys pressed against her hand before she dropped them in the purse. Her tea craving had vanished.

She sat on the couch and tilted her head toward the ceiling. "Okay, God, what's going on? What are you trying to tell me?"

She closed her eyes and waited for a sign as her thoughts sent her back to Sunday School. She saw the classroom and posters with Bible verses hanging on the wall. Hebrews 13:5 came in so clearly. *I will never leave you nor forsake you.*

The words warmed her soul, like a blanket sheltering her from a winter chill. The verse echoed in her mind and eventually spilled past her lips.

Over and over she said, "I will never leave you nor forsake you."

Anna pondered God's love, His compassion, and His promise to always be with her. Her nose began to tickle. She held back tears as joy filled her heart.

Her realization meant she had never been alone. God

had been with her the whole time. After Lydia's death and Andrew's rejection, He never left her side.

A second scripture came to her remembrance. *Cast all your cares upon Him because He loves you.*

God cared about her feelings. He cared about what she was going through, no matter how big or small. And He cared about the pending adoption.

Without hesitation, she went to her desk, booted up her laptop, and began typing. Her fingers flew over the keyboard. They barely kept up with the thoughts in her head. Her second wind kept her going for the next three hours.

Chapter Forty-Five

Five months felt like five years since Anna had submitted her application to the adoption agency.

She spent hours filling out paperwork that looked more like scholarly books. They requested information on everything under the sun, and then some. Although it pained her to admit, Stephanie had been right about one thing—money.

Disclosing an unemployed work status sent the red flag soaring. Her desire to adopt Jake and raise him in a loving home was moot. In the eyes of the law, financial stability played a big role. She needed a steady income, and quick.

Channel 3 News was the obvious choice. Picking up where she left off as the five o'clock producer would surely get the gossip mill churning about her failed venture, but Anna didn't care. Jake's wellbeing trumped her reputation.

But Sarah's caveat proved to be true.

"I was afraid this would happen," the news director said, informing Anna of her replacement.

"What about another news producer position? I'll take associate."

"Sorry, Anna, everything is filled, all the way down to the weekend morning producer."

"The assignment desk?" Her hopeful tone sounded desperate.

"Nope. Nothing."

Time ticked away. The traditional route of applying for jobs and playing the waiting game put her in the danger zone. She had to get aggressive. As the old adage went, "It's not what you know, it's who you know."

After a few phone calls and much persuasion, she landed a freelance writing position with *The Buffalo News*. She hadn't written a newspaper article since her college days at Ball State University, but she didn't have time to be picky.

Although a start, it wasn't a steady paycheck. Back to the phones she went.

More poking around led her to the communications department at Buffalo State where a professor was going on maternity leave. She jumped at the chance to fill her spot teaching Introduction to Journalism and News Writing.

Her two stints together equaled half her salary at Channel 3. But money was money. Flexible schedules from both positions gave her ample time to complete the necessary parent training sessions and home study—a rigorous series of meetings and interviews with Stephanie Grey.

Anna was granted visitation with Jake twice a week. They spent Sunday mornings at church followed by lunch and an outing of his choice. A movie, bowling, the arcade, or weather permitting, miniature golf.

Thursday nights were spent having dinner at Anna's apartment then youth group, where he'd become heavily involved in outreach events in the community. She assisted the other moms in the kitchen making snacks for the hungry teens.

Jake's grades skyrocketed, landing him on the honor roll two consecutive terms. He also joined "Clean Up the Community," a city-wide project where volunteers repainted graffiti-stricken buildings in Buffalo.

Anna was so proud of Jake, like a mother should feel about her son.

Chapter Forty Six

Anna tugged at the sleeve of her new black and white dress, pulling it back to sneak a look at her watch. She let out an exaggerated sigh and glanced at Henry sitting beside her. His gaze dropped in the direction of her restless leg. Immediately, she stopped shaking it.

Wearing a soft gray suit and classic white dress shirt, he casually crossed one leg over the other and slid his hand over his burgundy tie.

"There's nothing to be nervous about, Anna. This is the easy part."

"Easy for who?" she replied.

A twinge of friendly envy rose up inside of her. If only she could be as calm as Henry about the court hearing. It was the final phase in the adoption process but waiting on the legal system along with bureaucratic red tape and Stephanie Grey had stretched Anna's patience. She'd hounded the social worker with phone calls and emails requesting any crumb of information and always got the same curt response. "When I know, I'll let you know."

Then the answer she'd been waiting for finally came during a lecture she was giving on newspaper editing. Her cellphone vibrated on the desk and when she saw the number on the caller ID, she abruptly left the room of thirty students.

Anna's brief conversation with Stephanie included the day and time of the hearing and nothing more. She was so excited to finally hear some good news that when she returned to the classroom, she dismissed the group twenty minutes early.

Now that the hearing had finally come, she almost wished she was back to waiting. She checked her watch again and turned around when she thought she heard the door open.

"Don't worry, she'll be here," Henry said.

"It's 9:54."

"I know. It'll be fine."

"She should be here by now."

"There's no need to panic."

Anna blew an absurd sigh. "I'm not panicking."

He raised his eyebrow.

Her fingers fidgeted, and her voiced cracked. "Okay, maybe a little."

His stare said she was lying through her teeth.

"Okay, a lot! The hearing starts at ten."

"People as good as Julie Donavan don't have to be early. They don't even have to show up on time, they just have to win."

The lawyer came highly recommended from Sarah. Her perfect record for successful adoption cases in Western

New York put her in great demand for family court cases.

"By the way, how did you get her on such short notice?" Henry asked.

"Let's just say I'm not one for begging, but I made an exception."

He cocked his head to the side. "You want this kid bad."

"I've never wanted anything more in my life, Henry."

His warm smile melted away some of her anxiety. He placed his hand on top of hers, giving it a good squeeze when the door in the back of the courtroom swung open. In unison, they turned around and watched a woman in a royal blue suit and black heels making confident strides down the aisle.

Anna stood up to greet her lawyer.

The woman's expression guaranteed victory. "Good morning, Anna."

"Hi Julie." She shook her lawyer's hand, hoping her moist palm didn't expose her nerves.

The lawyer grinned, tucking a piece of brown hair behind her ear. "There's nothing to worry about. This is all a formality." She touched Anna's shoulder. "Trust me, in thirty minutes, you'll be walking out of this courtroom with your son."

"Thanks. I needed that."

Having a professional like Julie on her side took away some of the angst Anna felt.

"I'm a lawyer, I'm a counselor, it's all part of the job," she quipped, walking to the table near the bench. She opened her briefcase and removed Jake's file, a yellow legal pad, and a pen.

The courtroom door opened again only this time, tension filled the small room. It had to be Stephanie. Anna turned around as the social worker marched down the aisle and pointed her finger at a row, ordering Jake where to sit.

Anna smiled and waved at him, impressed with his choice of a red dress shirt, black tie, and black pants. It was a far cry from the ratty T-shirt and baggy jeans he'd worn the morning of his arraignment. And his hair! She chuckled thinking how his overgrown bangs had kept him from making eye contact with anyone.

The last time she was in a courtroom, Jake was headed for Wyatt Hall. But after today, he'd be going to a permanent home where he'd be loved unconditionally. No more bouncing from one foster family to the next.

The bailiff walked to the front of the bench. "All rise. The honorable Malcolm Forth presiding."

The portly judge entered the courtroom from a side entrance and sat down announcing, "Be seated." He was handed a manila folder and scanned the case file.

"We are here today to hear testimonies in the adoption case of Jacob David O'Connor to Anna Marie Sutton." He glanced up and addressed Anna's lawyer. "Ms. Julie Donovan is Miss Sutton's legal representative. Ms. Donovan, you may begin."

"Thank you, Your Honor. I call Judge Henry Rowland to the stand."

Henry stood up and smoothed out the burgundy tie for the second time. "Here we go," he said, patting Anna's shoulder.

He met the bailiff at the witness box where the court official held out a Bible. Henry held up his right hand and placed his left hand on the book.

The bailiff said, "Do you swear to tell the truth, the whole truth, and nothing but the truth, so help you God?"

"I do."

"Be seated."

Julie stood with her fingertips perched on the edge of the table. "Judge Rowland, how do you know Miss Sutton?"

He leaned forward and spoke into the pencil-thin microphone attached to the witness box. "Miss Sutton and my son Kyle dated for about two years."

"In that time, how well did you get to know Miss Sutton?"

"Very well."

"Please describe Miss Sutton's character."

Henry relaxed his posture. "That's an easy one. Dependable, trustworthy, compassionate, loving. Someone who genuinely cares."

"Judge Rowland, some people may deem your decision to send Jake with Miss Sutton to Indiana last year a bit, shall we say, unorthodox. Some may even go as far as criticizing your ruling. Would you explain why you did what you did?"

"Ms. Donavan, I've been a judge for a long time, going on twenty years. I've heard a lot, and I've seen a lot. And sometimes, I have no other choice than to trust my gut. This time was no different. So, to answer your question, I knew the kind of person Miss Sutton was, and I knew she would be the best influence on Jake."

The lawyer nodded. "Judge Rowland, one last question. Should Miss Sutton be granted adoption of Jake O'Connor?"

"Absolutely, without a doubt."

"Thank you, Judge Rowland. No more questions for this witness, Your Honor."

Judge Forth looked down at Henry through his glasses resting midway down his nose. "You may step down, Judge Rowland. Ms. Donavan, your next witness."

"Your Honor, I call Stephanie Grey to the stand."

Anna had been dreading Stephanie's testimony. The social worker was the most influential person in the case. The President of the United States could be up on the stand spewing out accolade after accolade, but in the end, it all came down to Stephanie. She had the power to make Anna look like a hero or a flop.

The bailiff swore her in. Julie remained at the table and began her questioning. "Ms. Grey, did you notice any changes in Jake when he returned from Indiana?"

Stephanie leaned forward and simply replied, "Yes" into the microphone.

"What were those changes?" The lawyer smiled. "And please be specific."

"His attitude. His behavior. His grades."

"Can you give some examples?"

"Manners, for one. He was more compliant, more punctual."

"Ms. Grey, you mentioned Jake's grades. Can you elaborate?"

"Jake was a straight D student. He never studied and never did his homework. He didn't care about school."

Stephanie's belittling tone made Anna want to jump out of her seat and go another round. She gripped the chair's arms and focused on getting through the hearing.

The social worker continued. "But this school year he got As and Bs."

"Is there anything you can tell us about his activities outside of school?"

"He has a part-time job, ironically at Allen's Corner Store where the *incident* happened."

Anna's lips pursed together and her chest heaved. Glancing across the room at Jake, the backhanded comments didn't seem to faze him. She took a breath. If a sixteen-year-old could keep his cool, she could too.

Stephanie continued. "He volunteers in the community. And, oh yeah, he goes to church every Sunday." She sounded as if it was most boring place on Earth.

Julie pointed to Anna. "Is that because of Miss Sutton?"

"She played a role."

"Ms. Grey, do you think Miss Sutton would make a good mom?"

"That's not for me to decide. I base my decisions on facts not feelings."

"Got that right," Anna muttered under her breath.

Julie continued her questioning. "Do you have children, Ms. Grey?"

"Yes. Two, a boy and a girl."

"Putting your profession as a social worker aside for a moment and looking at this case as a mother, do you think Miss Sutton is the right person to raise Jake?"

The clever lawyer made her best strategic move of the day. She took the most important question and made it personal by tugging on the parental heartstrings.

The courtroom went silent, waiting for Stephanie's reply. Seconds felt like hours. The anticipation was even too much for the judge.

"Ms. Grey?" he said looking down at her. "Please answer the question."

She sighed. "Speaking as a mother, I don't think there's a person out there more qualified to raise Jake than Anna Sutton."

"Thank you, Ms. Grey. Your Honor, I have no further questions for this witness."

Judge Forth dismissed Stephanie from the stand.

"Your Honor, I call Anna Sutton to the stand."

Henry leaned over and whispered in her ear, "You'll be fine."

Anna went to the stand where the bailiff waited to swear her in. She took her oath, sat down, and stared straight ahead at her lawyer.

"Miss Sutton, did you know Jake prior to the Allen's Corner Store robbery?"

She leaned forward to speak into the microphone. Her nerves got the best of her as she stammered, "I-I didn't know him personally, but I recognized him." A bit vague, but she waited for Julie to dig for more details.

"How did you recognize him?" she asked.

"When I was a producer at Channel 3 News, we aired his father's funeral. Jake was on some of the videotape."

"And you knew who he was right away?"

"No, not at first. When I was at the police station, Lieutenant Macalister told me about Officer O'Connor."

"Miss Sutton, what was your reaction when Judge Rowland wanted to send Jake with you to Indiana?"

Anna glanced at Henry and smiled. "Shocked. Caught off guard. To be honest, I didn't want Jake to come with me."

"Why?"

"I was going to Indiana to work on a project. I was writing a book. I just wanted to be alone."

"What changed your mind?"

"I felt sorry for him. I thought about him spending years at Wyatt, and even though some people believed it was the best solution, I didn't. We all do stupid things, Ms. Donovan. Things we regret and can't take back. But I believe in second chances, and Jake deserved a second chance. He's a good kid who got caught up with the wrong crowd."

"How did Jake act when you brought him to Indiana?"

"The first week was rough. He didn't want to be there, and he made sure I knew it. He had rules to follow, and he was staying with a stranger. I could see why he was angry. But, little by little, he adjusted."

"Miss Sutton, why do you want to adopt Jake?"

There it is was, the million-dollar question. The only question that really mattered.

"I know what it's like to lose a parent. It's the worst feeling in the world. It's not easy for an adult, and it sure isn't easy for a kid. Jake lost both his parents. He deserves a family and a home where he is loved. Albeit, our family will be small, but size doesn't matter. Numbers don't matter. It's about love."

"Miss Sutton, do you love Jake?"

Her eyes shifted in his direction. "Yes, and I want to be his mom."

Julie clasped her hands together. "No further questions for this witness, Your Honor," and she sat down.

The judge nodded for her to leave the stand. "You may take your seat, Miss Sutton."

Anna sighed with relief as she went back and sat down.

"Before I render my decision, I'd like to speak with Jake."

Malcolm Forth tilted his round face upward. "Son?" He waved his hand, motioning for the teen to come forward.

Jake turned to Stephanie seeking her permission. She nodded her head. He left his seat and looked across the courtroom at Anna as he made his way to the bench where the bailiff swore him in.

Judge Forth removed his glasses and swiveled his chair to the side facing the witness box. "Hey there, Jake. How are you doing?"

The teen looked up at the judge and quietly answered, "Good." He repeated, "Good," a bit louder into the mic.

"How did you feel when you found out Anna wanted to adopt you?"

"Really happy."

The judge leaned back. "Yeah? Why's that?"

"Well...because I'll be in a good home. I didn't like getting shuffled from one foster home to the next." His head hung. "No one's cared about me like this since my parents. Anna doesn't do anything she doesn't want to. So, if she is going through all this, I know she really cares. She's the real deal."

The judge nodded. "I see. So, Jake, I just have one more question for you. Do you want Anna to be your adoptive mother?"

He smiled. "Yes, Your Honor, more than anything."

"Thanks, Jake. You can take your seat."

Everyone in the courtroom had been questioned. Finally, the official decision was about to be announced. Months of waiting, filling out mounds of paperwork, and having to interact with Stephanie all came down to that very moment.

Swiveling his chair to face the audience, Judge Forth put his glasses on and skimmed through Jake's file.

"This is one of the most unique adoption cases I've seen in my years on the bench.

There are many factors to take into consideration when placing a minor in the care of a non-biological adult, and we always act in the best interest of the child."

Anna didn't like what she was hearing. His introduction sounded like a parent giving a reasonable explanation before dropping the bomb.

She looked to Henry, hoping for clarity, but he seemed perplexed, too.

"There is a bond between Miss Sutton and Mr. O'Connor that's more than obvious, although that's not reason enough to bring these two parties together."

For a second, Anna felt her heart stop beating. Where had she gone wrong? What did she say or not say?

"However."

However? However is good.

"Based on the testimonies heard today, I can't find a single reason to oppose this adoption. Therefore, I hereby grant full custody to Miss Anna Sutton. Congratulations, case dismissed."

After a swift bang of the gavel, Judge Forth closed the file and stepped down from the bench.

Unable to contain her emotion, Anna jumped out of her seat and hugged Henry. "Thank you for everything."

He patted her back. "Anything for you."

She shook her lawyer's hand, then met Jake in the middle of the aisle where they embraced each another.

"Well, I guess this is it," Stephanie said, slinging her purse over her shoulder. "Good luck, Jake." She patted him on the shoulder.

"Bye, Stephanie."

The social worker marched up the aisle and out the door.

Anna wrapped her arm around her son's shoulder. "Come on, let's go home."

Epilogue

One Year Later

Anna loaded the last plate in the dishwasher as Jake came in the kitchen.

"All set for your test?" she asked.

"Yep." He shoved his history book into his backpack and zipped the bag shut.

Jake had studied hard all week for his history exam—the final test of his senior year. He chugged what was left of his orange juice from breakfast and stacked the cup on the top rack of the dishwasher.

After Anna and Jake moved back to Garrison, she'd taken a position teaching journalism at her alma mater, Ball State University. As for a home, the cottage was the only place they'd wanted to live. She offered to buy it from the Hartmans, but they wouldn't hear of it.

Denny, Claire, and Carl pitched in to spruce the place up. Even Mavis came by on occasion to lend a helping hand. After months of renovations, the outdated cottage had been transformed into a modern home.

Denny put on a new roof and white vinyl siding. A stamped concrete porch replaced the rickety steps and a new double-seated porch swing swayed in the breeze. Anna didn't have a green thumb, but thankfully, Pastor Gill and a few teens from youth group knew a thing or two about landscaping and planted bushes and vibrant pink and purple flowering shrubs along the perimeter. The gravel driveway had been covered with a sleek blacktop surface complete with a basketball hoop off to the side.

Hardwood replaced the dull brown floors and a fresh coat of paint brought the walls to life. The family room doubled in size to make space for the new furniture, flat-screen television, and a dining room set next to the gourmet kitchen with solid oak cabinets, granite countertops, and stainless steel appliances. A second bathroom was added off of Jake's bedroom, along with a cozy den for Anna to write.

Jake looked at the kitchen clock and slung his backpack over his shoulder. "I better get going."

Anna followed him to the front door like she did every morning before he left for school. She held the door open. "Have a good day."

"Thanks, you too."

He abruptly stopped halfway out the door, turned around, and hugged her. "I love you, Mom."

"I love you too, Jake."

Anna watched her son's face light up when Melanie Thompson walked up the driveway.

"Morning, Miss Sutton," she called out, waving.

"Good Morning, Melanie."

Most girls wouldn't have waited, but Melanie was different. Although she'd been free to date any boy she wanted, she'd turned down every invitation knowing someday Jake would be back in Garrison.

Their futures looked bright. Both were accepted to Ball State University. Jake was awarded a scholarship in the fine arts department and Melanie planned on studying elementary education.

Back in the living room, surrounded by photos, a wave of nostalgia swept over Anna as she picked up each frame. Some were of Jake and his parents, others of her and her mother.

Tucked in the corner was a bookshelf with recent photos depicting Jake's new life in Garrison. His senior portrait, their first mother/son fishing trip to Patoka Lake, posing in the boat each holding up a bass—his catch much larger than hers. At the prom in a black tuxedo with Melanie on his arm, dazzling in an aqua blue, floor-length dress. And a sketch he'd drawn of her and Claire on the porch swing.

In the middle of all the photos stood Jake's birthday gift. The photo album with David O'Connor's police badge reminded her daily of God's unconditional love.

She'd tried running. She'd tried hiding. But He never gave up on her. Through disappointments and failures, He never left her side. To top it off, He sent her Jake.

The tea kettle whistled, and Anna went into the kitchen

to make a cup of green tea which she took into the den.

She sat at her desk, took a sip of tea, then placed the cup next to the framed photo Claire took of her and Jake at his party. On the opposite side of the computer was a picture of Anna and Lydia on her sixteenth birthday that she'd found in her photo album.

As she waited for her laptop to boot up, she picked up the signed contract for her first novel, *Return to Garrison.* As she opened an email from her editor and began working on the first round of edits, she smiled thinking back to the morning in Henry's chambers when he spoke about her making the best seller's list.

Her plan for the summer had crumbled, and she was so glad it had, because she liked this ending a whole lot better.

The End

Acknowledgements

Proverbs 3: 6 says to acknowledge the Lord in all your ways and He will direct your path. I couldn't have written this book without the leading and guidance of my Lord and Savior, Jesus Christ. Thank you, Father, for putting this story in my heart to share with and inspire those who read it.

Chad, you have gone above and beyond the title of supportive husband. Thank you for reading each chapter and giving feedback and thought-provoking changes. For always reminding me "when your book gets published" not "if your book gets published." I couldn't ask for a better partner in this incredible journey of life.

Lucas, every time I look at you, my heart swells up with joy at the young man you have become. To say I am proud of you is an understatement. Being your mom is one of the biggest rewards of my life. Thank you for your patience and understanding while I wrote this book.

To my parents, Charlie and Mary Jo Tribunella, your love and encouragement have made me into the person I am today. Thank you for your support and belief in me during one of the biggest adventures of my life—writing this book.

To my WDCX family, past and present. You've all encouraged me along the way without even knowing it. A special thanks to Emily Tenter and Keri Schopp, my fellow writers and dear friends. Words fail to express what your support has meant to me over the years. You've both propelled me to keep going when I wanted to give up and replenished my hope in reminding me of what I was meant to do. I will always treasure our time together. To Brett Larson, to this day, handing you a script twists my stomach into a knot. Suddenly, I'm back in college waiting for the professor to click the red pen. But with every critique, I learned something new. Thanks for not holding back. In doing so, it showed you cared enough to make me the best writer I can be.

To Sarah Warner, my high school locker neighbor for four years, I wouldn't have known about emergency foster care policies and youth detention centers without your insight and knowledge. Thank you. And Sarah, go ahead and tell everyone about this book!

Kristy Tasca, you have an amazing talent and gift for photography. My photos still blow me away. Thank you for making me feel like a supermodel.

A big thank you to Melissa Secchiaroli. When you agreed to design my website, a huge weight was lifted off my shoulders. You have a good eye for detail, and I value your insight and creativity. Thank you for capturing what I could never express.

ABOUT THE AUTHOR

 Kari Wirth has a master's degree in journalism from Ball State University and more than twenty years of experience working in the media. She is currently an executive writer/producer for a Christian radio company. She is always working on a new project but still manages to find time to read, bake, work out, and is an avid 5K runner. Kari resides in Lockport, New York, with her husband and their son.

MORE CONTEMPORARY CHRISTIAN NOVELS FROM JOURNEY FICTION

FINDING MISS WRITE

Gena Webb - The Misadventures of Miss Write, Book 1
When suspense novelist Carla Williams is accused of planning an actual murder, her life takes on more plot twists than one of her books. Sure, her life's in danger, but she's also caught the attention of handsome detective, Roger Graf, so that kind of evens things out.
As Carla nears the end of her novel, will Roger stop the killer, or will it be the end of Carla's life story as well?

THE WRITE DECISION

Gena Webb - The Misadventures of Miss Write, Book 2
When Carla Williams lands on the jury of a high-profile attempted murder case, she looks forward to some in-the-field research. Her police detective fiancé, Roger, would never ask her to compromise her principles, but will he support her when she sides with the defendant and starts her own investigation to find the real shooter? Will Carla still get her happy ending, or has she stumbled into a plot twist she can't write her way out of?

ONE INNER VOICE

Kay Wyont - Alamo City Mystery, Book 1
San Antonio Police Detectives Randy Monroe and Danny Beckman know two things: a serial killer is on the loose, and they don't have enough clues to catch him. Surely the fact that the victims are murdered elsewhere and the bodies dumped at churches means something, but what? With every new incident, Randy and Danny become more obsessed with unraveling the facts. But the closer they get to the truth, the more it looks like it might take a miracle to bring the killer to justice.

TAKE A TRIP THROUGH
TIME WITH JOURNEY FICTION

A Worthy Suitor

Jennifer AlLee

Reluctant socialite Gwendolyn Banks is happier in the woods surrounding Tuxedo Park than attending the vibrant parties hosted there. But after stumbling upon accomplished archer Albert Taylor, she reconsiders her life of solitude.

The Counterfeit Clue

Lisa Karon Richardson

When Gemma Gaines sees her friend killed in a hit-and-run, all her instincts tell her it was no accident. With the doggedness of the great Girl Detective herself, and the help of a handsome new neighbor – who may be more than he seems – she's soon on the trail of a counterfeiting ring that would like nothing more than to put her out of circulation for good.

Cassandra and the Cowboy

Janine Mick Wills

When enigmatic cowboy Matt Atkins shows up looking for a job at the Triple P Ranch, he convinces Cassandra Pickett that he'll be an asset. As they work side by side, Cassandra's feelings for Matt deepen. But her dreams are shattered when she discovers that Matt harbors a hidden agenda for the Triple P. Will Cassandra have to turn to her neighbor and a marriage of convenience, or will God take the shards of her broken dreams and create something beyond what she dared hope for?

Made in the USA
Middletown, DE
20 October 2020